WALK THE LINE

A HIDDEN OASIS NOVELLA

HARLOW LAYNE

GAGE

Adrenaline pulsed through my veins as I arrived on scene and the carnage that was laid out in front of me. Three cars were totaled, and debris littered the road. The smell of burnt rubber still permeated the air as I stepped out of the car. I paid no attention to where my partner went as I leapt out of the cruiser.

I barely took two steps before Dave Rogers, a fellow officer, barked out a command as he raced over to one of the three cars. "Walker, you're needed at the vehicle that went down the embankment. The other fire trucks are at a house fire and we're all hands-on deck."

"Fuck," I swore under my breath. I knew that embankment and it was steep as fuck. Whoever went over would be lucky to be alive.

The one bad thing about living in a relatively small town were scenes like this one. We had limited resources and were spread thin when multiple situations occurred. It didn't happen often. Luckily.

As I started down the hill and tried not to slide the whole way on my ass, I heard shouts and a couple of cheers. "She's alive."

My steps quickened. I knew they would need as many hands as they could get as I took in the car. I couldn't even make out the model it was so smashed up. It looked like a ball of crushed up red metal. The vehicle had rolled at least three times before a tree stopped its descent.

"Walker talk to the victim and try to keep her awake. She keeps falling in and out of consciousness. It's going to take us a few minutes to get that door open and her out." One of the rescue workers barked at me. I couldn't make out who he was as he ducked low to get a better look at the vehicle.

The first thing I noticed about her was her fiery red hair as her head sagged against the window frame. Her body was covered in dirt, tinged with blood from the gash on her forehead and various other places. One arm was broken and who knew what else. She'd be lucky to get away with only one broken bone.

Lightly placing my hand on her shoulder, I asked her. "Ma'am, can you hear me?" She stirred but her eyes stayed closed even as I saw movement underneath her pale eyelids. "Can you tell me your name?"

Slowly opening her eyes, she blinked her big gray eyes at me. "Ma'am, you've been in a car wreck. We're working on getting you out, but in the meantime try not to move around too much. Can you do that for me?"

Her eyes darted around as she took in the broken glass all over her lap and all around her. The hood was crushed up to the steering wheel. All the entry ways had been mashed with each impact as she rolled down the hill. She was lucky to be alive. "What happened?" Her voice bordered on hysteria as tears welled in her eyes.

"All I know is there was a multi-car accident and you were a part of it. Rescue is working to get you out of your car and then you'll be transported to the local hospital. Do you remember anything about the incident?"

"I remember... being hit from the side. It came out of nowhere," she whispered as tears started to trail down her dirty cheeks.

"I'm sure that must have been scary for you, but you're safe now and they'll have you out of there in no time."

Her eyes started to close, and her head fell back against the headrest.

"Ma'am, I need you to stay awake. Do you know your name?" I asked again.

She blinked up at me with a silly smile on her face. Her eyelids fluttered shut. "I must be dreaming."

"Why do you say that?" I asked loudly over the sounds of the saw against metal. Only a couple more minutes and they'd have the door removed and her quickly on the way to the hospital.

Slowly her gray eyes opened and crinkled at the sides. "You look like that guy who plays Superman. Oh my God, are you Henry..." She looked down and then back up at me. "Shit why can't I remember his last name?"

Internally I rolled my eyes, but I didn't let my irritation show. I was used to people commenting on who I looked like.

"I hate to let you down, but no, I'm not him. Although my twin brother and I get asked that question a lot. Him even more so."

"Why?" She murmured, leaning her head back on the head rest and looking me over.

"Because he wears thick black framed glasses just like Clark Kent."

"Is his name Clark?" She smiled sweetly and even underneath all the dirt and blood, she shined.

"No, it's Tate." I answered with a smile. Tate hated all the women who went goo-goo over his Clark Kent looks.

Her head started to list to the side, eyes closing.

"What's your name?" This time I was asking for myself.

"Claire."

"Nice to meet you Claire, I'm Gage. Only a couple more minutes and we'll have you out of here."

"Good because I need to get to work." She looked down at herself and frowned. "Do you think I'll make it into work today?"

"Not today. First you have to go to the hospital and get checked out. You probably have a concussion." *Or more.*

Claire's face started to crumble. Her right hand rose to touch her left arm but pulled back at the last second. Looking down, she frowned. "My arm hurts. A lot. I think it might be broken."

"I think so too sweetheart, but one broken bone for as bad of a wreck you were in isn't bad at all."

"I can't even wipe my tears," she whimpered.

Reaching inside, my thumb brushed under one eye and then the other. Claire watched intently as I worked to rid her face of tears and grime. "Is that better?"

"Yes, thank you. Does your brother have tattoos like you?" Claire eyed my arms appreciatively. I had tattoos down to my wrists on both arms.

"Not a one. That way people can distinguish us if he doesn't have his glasses on." Tate hated tattoos and every single one that I had on my body. Nor did we have the same eyes, but you had to really look to notice the difference. I hated it. Always had so I wasn't going to tell her what made me different from almost everyone I'd ever encountered.

"So, are you the bad boy brother?" She asked with a slight smile until the metal screeched loudly from the rescue workers trying to open her door. Her face paled to the point I thought she might lose consciousness

"Stay with me Claire. I promise there's nothing to be afraid of. They're only working to get you out of there."

"Stay with me!" She implored, desperately. Her gray eyes turning as dark as an impending storm.

"I'm not going anywhere." I responded calmly hoping it would help alleviate Claire of her sudden anxiety.

"You promise to stay with me?" Her gaze stayed trained on my own as workers moved in to cut her seatbelt away.

"There's no need to be afraid. I promise I'll stay right by your side."

"Okay," she whispered. She blinked back more tears as her chin trembled. I hated seeing her scared. Claire watched as two rescue workers worked in tandem to release her legs that were pinned.

"This is going to hurt." One of them announced a second before releasing her legs.

Claire screamed out in pain; tears tracked down her cheeks like rain in a spring shower. Her already pale face grew even paler.

"We've got to move. She's bleeding from her femoral artery," the other rescuer shouted.

I started to yell out for help when a stretcher and EMT crashed down the hill. *Fuck! We were going to have a hell of a time getting her back up that embankment.*

Everything after that happened in a matter of seconds and a lifetime all at once. I stood back out of the way as they got Claire onto the stretcher and started up the hill.

"Gage," she called, her voice frightened.

Jogging up to Claire, I picked up her hand and squeezed. "I'm right here." With my other hand, I helped pushed the stretcher up the hill. I was pleased to see they'd attached a rope in case anyone slipped. We were lucky it wasn't raining. Not that it rained much in Oasis. If the ground had been wet, it would have taken too long to get Claire out of there.

As we came closer to the ambulance, I started to release Claire's hand, but she only held it tighter. Smiling down at her, I tried to speak calmly enough to soothe her. "Claire, you've got to let go now so they can put you in the ambulance. The EMT's need to take care of you."

"But you said you'd stay by my side. I don't want to be alone," her lower lip quivered.

"You won't be alone. All these nice people are going to help you and give you the best care you can get."

"I don't know them. I want you to come with me."

Why was she reacting so irrationally? I'd never met her before today.

"Please." A tear slipped down her cheek as she reached out for me.

What was I doing?

"Sure," I answered as I stepped up into the ambulance with her. I paid no mind to the looks the EMT's were giving me. There was something about Claire that made it impossible for me to say no to. I just didn't know what.

$$\frac{2}{}$$

GAGE

My head bowed with my elbows resting on my knees, hands hanging between my legs. I'd been sitting in this hard-plastic waiting room chair for the last two hours waiting on any word about Claire.

A pair of black tactical boots came to stand in my line of sight. "Dude, why are you still here?" Steve Allen's nasally voice asked.

Rolling my head to the side, I saw his stupid cocky grin that was always on his face. I wanted nothing more than to punch it right off. I'm not sure what his problem was but he'd had out for me since he was transferred to the Oasis police department a couple of years ago.

Sitting back, I stared up at Steve giving him nothing. "I'm a man of my word and I told Claire I'd be here when the doctors were through examining her after she nearly lost her shit when they tried to separate us."

The douchebag rolled his eyes at me, his thumbs hooked through the belt loops of his pants as he looked down at me. "You've got a stage five clinger. If I was you, I'd get out now while you still can."

I scoffed. Why couldn't he leave me the hell alone? "Well, thank God I'm not you. What are you doing here anyway? Are you that desperate you're trolling the hospital waiting rooms for dates?"

"Funny, Walker. When are you going to make detective like your brother? Or are you not smart enough?" He sneered, making me want to punch him in the face.

"He does his thing and I do mine. Don't worry about us." Luckily for me, my phone rang with my detective brother's ringtone. Maybe our twin thing let him know I was talking about him or I was about to do something that would get me in trouble. Pulling my phone from my pocket, I hit the green answer button. "What's up baby bro?"

"Where are you?" Tate's voice was off. Something was bothering him.

"At the hospital. Why?"

"Are you okay? You weren't hurt were you?" he paused, but not long enough for me to answer him. "What are you doing at the hospital?"

"I'm fine. You'd know if I was hurt or not." Jeez, you'd think he was the one older by seven minutes with the way he smothered me sometimes.

"We can't count on our twin ESP," he scoffed. Tate was the easy going one of the two of us and mostly let my shit fly. Tonight, he wasn't, and I was going to find out why.

"I was called to a scene. A gnarly multi-car wreck and one of the vics was down that steep as fuck embankment. You know the one I'm talking about?"

"Fuck, yeah. Not one I'd want to be stuck down in."

"Right. Me either. She… got attached and begged me to stay with her so here I am in the ER waiting room while she gets checked out. Once I can go back and see her, I'll head out. I'm going to need you to pick me up." A loud sigh worked its way through the speaker. Tate was annoyed, but he'd pick me up. He'd do anything for me the same way I'd do anything for him. "What did you call about? I'm sure it wasn't about my day."

"We've got another dead body." Tate growled. He'd been working on a couple of murder cases with no luck and this made three. A serial.

"I'm assuming it's the same M.O.?" I noticed Allen was still standing close to me listening. Pushing up, I shoulder checked him as I went to the other side of the room where he couldn't hear me speak.

"Fuck, Gage," he sighed heavily into the phone like the weight of the world was on his shoulders. "You know what this means."

Unfortunately, I did.

"Any leads?"

"What do you think?" He sounded defeated and I hated that. My brother was a good man and took his work to heart, never giving up. I could picture Tate taking off his glasses and pinching the bridge of his nose. He was smart. Smarter than most. A hell of a lot smarter than me which is what made him such a great detective and I knew it was killing him that someone was out there and had killed three women. I also knew he wouldn't sleep until he caught whoever it was.

"I think you won't stop until you've found him, and the people of Oasis are safe." I was proud of my brother. He had become the youngest detective on our force at twenty-eight, everyone respected and went to him when they couldn't figure out a crime scene.

We were quiet for a moment. I knew he was going over every detail in his head and I was thinking about when they'd finally let me talk to Claire for a minute. I hoped she didn't freak out again because there was no way in hell, I was spending the night at the hospital.

"Let me know when you want me to pick you up. We'll grab some food and beer— "

"And hash out the case." I interrupted. I might not have been an official detective, but I did know a thing or two, and Tate liked to use me as a new set of eyes to see if he missed anything.

"It's the least you can do for making me pick you up. I hope she's worth it," he chuckled before he hung up.

Was Claire worth it? I didn't know. Did I even want her?

Noticing Allen had left the waiting room, I sat back down in the seat I'd occupied before. Resting my head back against the wall, I closed my eyes. I knew Tate would likely keep me up half the night going over evidence and any theories he had and wanted to get some shut eye while I could.

"Officer Walker?" I heard called from far away. Squinting open my left eye; I saw a woman in blue scrubs standing in front of me. She was short with bright purple glasses and a no nonsense look on her face.

I guessed I'd fallen asleep.

"Yes?" I cleared my throat and stood. "Is the victim…" Had I not asked Claire her last name? "Alright?"

A smile she must have used at least a hundred times a day tipped her lips. "Ms. Blake is stable and asking to see you. If you'll follow me, I'll take you back so we can continue treatment."

"Is she refusing treatment?"

Maybe Claire really was a stage five clinger.

"We need to take her upstairs for a CT scan to make sure she doesn't have any internal bleeding then put a cast on her arm. She said you were on scene with her?"

I wasn't sure why the nurse said it as a question.

"One of a couple dozen, but yeah, I was the one who tried to keep her calm and awake. Why?"

"No reason. Ms. Blake is very adamant she speaks to you before we take her up that's all. I'm sure I don't have to tell you this, but sometimes when people are in a stressful situation with someone else, they bond to that person. The way she's demanding to see you… it seemed like you two knew each other beforehand." Her eyes flicked to me and then back to watching where we were going.

"It's never happened to me before," I chuckled warily. "She was quite upset when I tried to leave her side." That was an understatement, but it felt wrong to tell the nurse how Claire had cried and started to sob when I stepped away. If the arm closest to me hadn't been broken I was sure she would have grabbed onto me and never let go.

The nurse looked at me as if she knew I was underplaying how badly it had gone. "If it happens again, we can sedate her. We'll need her calm."

Running a hand through my hair, I murmured. "Hopefully it doesn't come to that."

"Let's hope," she snipped.

What crawled up her ass all of a sudden?

We stopped in front of a door and I could see Claire in her hospital bed through the window. She looked so tiny and sad as she stared at the plain white hospital wall. Even from this far away I could see the tear streaks that had made their way down her ivory cheeks through all the dirt and blood.

The moment the door to her room opened and Claire saw me, her eyes shined with tears. "You stayed," she whispered relieved.

Standing at the end of her bed, I smiled down at her. Even with dirt and blood all over her and her hair caked to the side of her head, Claire was beautiful. I couldn't imagine what she'd look like cleaned up and ready for a date.

A date?

Shaking my head to get rid of my thoughts, I swallowed down my crazy thoughts. "I told you I would and I'm a man of my word. The nurse said you wanted to see me before they take you upstairs."

"Yes." Tears filled her big gray eyes. "I'm sorry I asked you to stay. I… I didn't realize—"

"It's okay." She started to speak but stopped when I raised my hand that still had her blood on it. Her face paled and instantly I clasped my hands behind my back. "Really it's okay. I didn't mind waiting. I wanted to make sure you were okay."

"That's very sweet of you. Do you do this kind of thing often?"

It didn't escape my notice when the nurse who'd brought me in seemed to take interest in our conversation.

"What kind of thing?"

"Saving women and escorting them to the hospital to then wait in the ER for them," she answered quietly. I swore I saw a blush underneath all the dirt.

"The only people I escort to the hospital are when they've been injured and have been arrested, so no I don't make a habit of accompanying pretty ladies to the ER."

"They said I have to stay the night for observation and I'm sure you must be tired. I wanted to thank you for…everything." Her voice hitched at the end.

"You don't have to thank me. I'm only doing my job." I lightly patted her leg and watched as a little of the light dimmed in her eyes. "Do you have anyone you need to contact? I can do that for you before I go."

Biting her plump bottom lip, she shook her head.

"I've got no one. Just my work, but you don't need to call them. One of the nurses said they'd do it earlier."

Fishing my wallet out of my back pocket, I pulled one of my business cards out and sat it on the table beside her bed. "If you need anything like a ride home tomorrow, my cell number is on the back."

Her big gray eyes blinked up at me, shining bright. "Thank you, Gage. I might just do that."

I nodded and saw the nurse smirk over in the corner as I walked to the door.

What was I doing giving her my number and telling her I'd take her home? I must have lost my mind somewhere at the bottom of that embankment.

3

GAGE

Slumping back into Tate's Wrangler's seat, I rolled my head back. He had the top and sides off like he normally did, and I took advantage and stared up into the starry night as he started to drive away from the hospital.

"You look like shit." Tate laughed, tapping his thumbs to the beat of whatever shit music he was listening to. We may have always looked the same, but we'd never had the same taste in music. His sounded like hippie-dippie music. I tried to block it out and focus on the wind and sky above.

"Thanks. You don't look too great yourself. When's the last time you slept more than a couple of hours?"

Tate kept quiet with his eyes trained on the road and didn't speak again until he was pulling outside one of the best taco trucks in the city. "How many?" He grunted out as he hopped out of the Jeep.

Since I couldn't remember if I'd even ate that day, I waved four fingers. "I'll get the beer."

"If you want." He gave me a chin lift and made his way to the line. Luckily there were only a few people this late at night. Manny's was normally packed with a line twenty deep.

I continued to stare up at the night sky while I waited. Every time I closed my eyes, I saw Claire pinned helplessly in her car with dirt and blood all over her. *Why was she affecting me so?*

"You want to tell me about it?" Tate asked as he slid back inside, handing me the bag full of tacos. The spicy aroma hitting my nose made my stomach growl.

"Nah, I don't… I just can't seem to get her out of my head."

"That's not a bad thing, Gage." He sounded tired. Part of it was the case, but I knew the other part was Tate wanted to find someone to spend his life with. The problem was he never seemed to find the right girl. At one point, I thought he might be gay. Hell, he might be. I didn't know because that was one thing Tate never spoke to me about. EVER.

"Do you have someone you can't get off your mind?" I asked, probing.

His eyes flicked to look over at me. "I have three women on my mind. Three that are dead."

Dead. Dead. Dead.

Not what I had in mind when I asked him, but I knew he wouldn't answer me.

Pulling up in front of the gas station, I waited until he put the Jeep in park. "Don't you think it would be good to have someone to share your work with?"

"I have you," he answered gruffly. He rolled his eyes but then turned to look at me with a flash of confusion.

"Of course, you have me. You'll always have me. You can't get rid of me that easily, but don't you want to have someone there waiting for you at home. Someone you can tell everything?"

"Are you behind on your rent? Do you need to move in?" He asked dead serious, but I saw his lips twitch.

"Oh my God, Tate," I slammed my head back against the head rest. "Don't be a dick. I'm not talking about me."

"I get you got some girl under your skin but don't start this shit with me. It's not going to work and no, I don't want someone to share my work with. There's no way in hell I'd tell a girlfriend or wife the things I see day in and day out." His brows furrowed; lips tipped down. "You would?"

I scoffed and pushed his shoulder. "Not everything,

but I don't see the shit you see. What's the harm in telling about how stupidly someone tried to get out of a traffic ticket?"

"I doubt any girlfriend is going to want to hear how some chick showed you her boobs to get out of a traffic ticket," he chuckled darkly. He was probably right about that, but there were other things I could share. Other things he could share if he wanted to. "Now are you going to buy the beer or are you giving me shit so I'll buy it?" He turned off the Jeep, ready to get out and stop our conversation.

"I'll get it, jackass," I unbuckled my seatbelt. "But there's nothing wrong with wanting or having a companion."

"I didn't say there was," he snapped, glaring at me. "Drop it, Gage and get us some beer."

"Fine," I growled back. "But I don't want you asking about this chick either."

"Fine," he drawled out with irritation ringing clear. Fuck he was annoying, but I loved him.

I headed to the back of the store and snagged a twelve pack of Heineken out of the cooler. I'd leave what we didn't finish at his place for another time. I wasn't much of a drinker. Neither of us were but some-times we liked to kick back a couple and relax while we caught up. While standing in line to check out, I swore I felt my phone go off, but when I looked at it there were no notifications. Immediately my thoughts went to Claire and if they found any internal bleeding, and if she lost it after I left.

Placing the beer on the floorboard. Tate shifted into drive, headed toward his house. He didn't live far, and traffic was light late at night, so it only took us a few minutes. Pulling into the garage, he eyed the beer. "I see you didn't go with the cheap stuff."

I shrugged. "You seem stressed."

"You didn't need to, but thanks." One side of his mouth tipped up. He grabbed a roll of paper towels and a bottle opener as we made our way through his kitchen and into his living room. Placing our food on the coffee table, he sat down on the couch and picked up the remote. "Did you watch last night's game?"

"Nah, I was working. Pull it up." Flipping the caps off two beers, I sighed as the cool tip met my lips. I took a long swallow before I took in the twelve tacos stacked on the table. Tate either hadn't listened or he was ravenous. "Hungry?" I guffawed.

"Jesus, Gage, chill out. You know you always want more than you order and yeah, I'm fucking hungry. I've had shit food for the last two days and I want to indulge in my favorite tacos. Sue me. Now stuff your mouth or I'll stuff it for you." Tate took a long pull from his beer, his eyes in slits as he watched me take my first bite.

It seemed like I needed to lay off my brother or

we'd be on the floor wrestling and beating the shit out of each other in a matter of minutes. "Sorry, bro. We've both had a long day or three. Thanks for the tacos. I can't remember the last time I had Manny's."

He nodded and yawned. Only then did I notice the purple slashes under his eyes. It had been a few days since we last talked and if I had to guess that was the last time Tate had slept more than an hour or two here and there. I felt like shit for not answering his call a couple of nights ago. Maybe if I had he would have talked to me.

"Have you talked to mom lately?"

I shoved the rest of the taco in my mouth so I wouldn't have to answer the question.

"Fuck man, you know we're all she has."

I knew and now I felt like a crap brother and son. Our dad skipped out on our mom when we were two months old. He couldn't handle the fact that our mom (who's the best fucking mom in the world) couldn't dedicate her life only to him any longer. I couldn't imagine what it must have been like to raise twin boys alone. Once we got older, we were hellions. On a good day.

"Is she okay?"

Tate tilted his head in my direction. He knew it had been too long since I'd picked up the phone or visited. I was lousy at communication. I thought to call at the most inopportune moments. Once I got home from a shift, I was usually tired and all I wanted to do was throw myself on my bed and sleep.

"She misses you. Us. She wants us to come visit soon. Maybe the next time you have a couple of days off, let me know and I'll see if I can work something out and we can head up there." He frowned and it made the dark smudges underneath his eyes stand out more.

"She'd love that… and we could both use the break. Get out of town and chill."

"Just let me know when. I hate that she's hours away and all alone. I wish I could convince her to move down here, but she hates the heat."

"Don't we all," I laughed, and Tate followed along with me. The summers were brutal, but the weather for the rest of the year made up for those few months of torture. "If you *ever* need to talk—"

"I know and the same goes for you. Don't be such a stranger. Especially to your family. You know that no matter what I will always be there for you. Good or bad. I'd walk through fire for you. Take a bullet or give my last breath if it meant it would save you."

Fuck. I knew but hearing it made my chest burn with emotion.

"I know baby bro and the same goes for you. I'm just not as articulate as you are, but you feel me," I choked out. Taking a pull from my beer, I turned to the game.

"I feel you, Gage."

<hr>

THE BUZZING AND CHIRP OF MY PHONE PULLED ME FROM a deep haze. I looked around to see Tate asleep, sprawled out on the couch with one arm thrown over his face. I guess it was a good thing I'd taken the recliner.

Grabbing my phone from the table an unknown number appeared on the display. Swiping, I answered. My voice was rough from being asleep for however long.

"Hello? Gage?" A sweet female voice asked.

"Here," I yawned.

"Oh… you sound different. Did I wake you?" She sounded surprised.

"Yeah," I yawned again and looked toward the window. Tate had blinds that he left closed most of the time to keep out the sun and heat, but through a little crack I could see that it was daylight outside. Bright daylight. "What time is it?"

"A little after one… in the afternoon. You must have been up late. I'm sorry I shouldn't have called you."

"Are you being released soon?"

"As soon as the nurse comes back, but don't worry about it. I can get an Uber—"

"I said I'd give you a lift and I'm a man of my word."

"You keep telling me that. Thanks, Gage, but if it's too much—"

"I wouldn't have offered." And I wanted to see her again. Maybe then I could figure out why I couldn't get her out of my head.

Claire spoke so softly, I felt like I had to be Superman to hear what she said next. "You might be the last man of his word left."

If she only knew.

Tate turned so his back was to me. He let out a puff of air and I knew he was back to sleep. I'd write him a note to thank him for last night.

We'd fallen asleep during the game. The TV was off, so he probably turned it off at some point and laid down on the couch. I was surprised he hadn't gotten up and went to bed. I then noticed I had a blanket draped over me.

Instead of me being there for my brother, he had taken care of me.

"I'll be right there."

4
———

CLAIRE

I sat outside the hospital in the wheelchair I'd been wheeled down in feeling like a fool. Why had I called that hot cop? Surely, he had better things to do on a Saturday afternoon like go to the gym and add more muscles to his already bulging body or get another tattoo.

Or be with his girlfriend.

I didn't want to think about him with another woman even though I had no claim on him in anyway.

Instead of sitting there like a loser, I should've called Aja. She would have picked me up and then probably would've forced me to her apartment where she'd mother me to death. Yeah that's why I didn't call her and besides the people I worked with I didn't have any other friends after moving from my hometown of Olympia.

A shiny metallic blue Jeep pulled up in the loading and unloading zone right in front of me. The poor nurse that was stuck waiting with me was probably tired of being out in the heat when she could be inside the freezing hospital. She wasn't much of a talker otherwise I would have tried to fill the silence with some chitchat. I was not looking forward to having to ask her if I could borrow her phone and call Aja.

My jaw hit the sidewalk when Gage walked around the back with a sexy swagger. He was dressed in all black. Each item of clothing fit him like a glove showcasing every asset he had to offer. The sleeves of his t-shirt hit his biceps showing the defined muscles and his inked arms while his tight as sin jeans hugged his toned ass. I'd never been an ass woman, but I'd give anything to sink my teeth into those globes. I knew he'd be the star of my dreams for weeks to come and who'd I'd think about as I pleasured myself. He was perfection.

"Have you been down here long?" His deep voice rumbled affecting my lady bits.

"Oh no, only a couple of minutes." The nurse all but cooed at him. She shimmied around me to stand between us, fluffing her hair.

Gage frowned down at her. "Do I need to sign something for Claire to be released?"

"Claire?" Her voice was high and uncertain.

Had she really forgotten I was there?

I wanted to say something bitchy because seriously who the hell did she think she was. Did she really think he saw her from the street and had to come meet her? Or did they already know each other?

I grimaced as I stood up and the stitches from my leg wound stretched. My body felt as if a semi had run over it and then decided to back over me for good measure. "Do you two know each other?"

"No," he replied gruffly. His brows pulled together as he took me in. Moving to my side, Gage's warm hand wrapped around my right upper arm that wasn't broken as he helped me to the Jeep. "I'm sorry I wasn't really thinking when I came to get you." One side of his mouth tipped down. "Let me help you up."

After making sure I was situated and comfortable which wasn't exactly easy to maneuver with a heavily swollen knee on one leg and the other leg with stitches, Gage ran around to the driver side and hopped in.

"Again, I'm sorry about the Jeep," he started it up. "I was at my brother's when you called—"

"No need to apologize. I'm sorry I called and interrupted your… sleep." I had wanted to say day, but I remembered that he'd been asleep when I called. I started to say more, but his phone rang through the speakers. I wanted to know why he was at his brother's house and asleep. Never had I been this noisy before in my life, but I wanted to know everything about him.

"Hey bro, you're up," he winked over at me with a devilish smile on his face.

"Where's my Jeep, Gage?" A voice almost exactly the same as the man sitting next to me boomed out. It was deep and surprisingly soothing for how angry he sounded.

"About that… Claire called, and I had to pick her up from the hospital. I'm going to bring it back after—"

"You need to bring it back now. I have to get back to the station. Swing by and pick me up, you can grab your car at the station."

"I really think I should get Claire home and then—"

"No and then…" his brother grumbled. "If you don't remember, I need to catch a murderer. Get your ass over here—"

"Gage," I spoke quietly as I interjected. "I really don't mind if you need to pick up your brother. I don't have anything pressing to get home to."

He slowed down, turning on the turn signal. "Are you sure? I have to believe you'd be much more comfortable at home in your nice comfy bed."

"It's very sweet of you to be concerned about me, but your brother has a much more pressing matter."

"Fine, asshole. You better be ready to go when we get there," he growled out. Even though he was pissed at his brother, listening to him talk was hot as hell.

"*You* don't be an asshole. "His brother growled back and then hung up.

As hot as it was, I felt bad for being the cause of them fighting. We sat in an uncomfortable silence through two lights before I couldn't take it anymore. I hated feeling the tension that was vibrating from the other side of the vehicle.

"Why did you take your brother's car?"

Gage cleared his throat, looking over at me. "What?"

I asked again only this time his blazing blue eyes were focused solely on me before the light changed.

Turning his gaze back to the road, he answered. "You asked me to come with you to the hospital, so my partner took the squad car back to the station. My brother wanted to catch up and go over… stuff so he picked me up last night when I left. We fell asleep watching a game and then you called. From there you know the rest."

My face heated along with my chest all the way up to my ears. "I feel like a burden. You could have said no at any time. I don't normally freak out like that."

Tilting his head to the side, he smiled. It was dazzling as was he. "Have you been in a wreck like that before?"

"I've never been in any kind of wreck let alone one of that magnitude. This is my first broken bone in twenty-four years of life." I looked down at my left arm. "Now I can check both off my life list."

"Life list?" He inquired.

"You know all the big and little things that happen during life." He raised a brow, so I continued. "You know like learn to ride a bike, swim, fly in an airplane, have your first kiss, or break a bone."

"Lose your virginity?" His wide smile showed off his straight white teeth that gleamed in the sunlight. Who knew even teeth could be sexy? I sure as hell didn't until Gage pointed his smile directly at me. I tried to shake off how he affected me. It would do me no good to have a crush on him.

My cheeks flamed. "That too."

"A bucket list," he stated.

"Yes," I shrugged to each their own. "I call it my life list."

"So has losing your virginity been checked off?" His smile was wicked as he looked over at me with utter curiousness.

Seriously was his mission in life to make me blush? I'd blushed more in the few minutes we'd been together then I had in the last ten years combined. "Yes, has yours?" I knew there was no way in hell he was a virgin, but even though the way he asked was flirty it was still rude. I wasn't going to tell him I'd only ever been with one person in all my twenty-four years.

Gage pushed his sunglasses down his nose to look at me, my blue eyes twinkling. "A very long time ago."

With his sunglasses down, I got a good look at his eyes and was shocked to see the left was blue and brown. "Your eyes are different colors. Are your brother's that why as well?"

"No," he slipped his shades back up and answered bitterly. "Only me."

"His loss. I'm sure he's jealous."

"Jealous," he scoffed. "Right. I was the one who always felt… why am I telling you this?" His knuckles turned white as he gripped the steering wheel tighter.

"I don't know, but I like to listen to you talk. How did it make you feel?"

"I've never been one to express my feelings to others," he grumbled. "Tate knew because… we just know stuff about each other. Twin ESP or whatever."

"If you don't want to tell me you don't have to, but I'm here if you want someone to listen." I was being honest when I said his brother might be jealous because it was seriously awesome. Had others made fun of him for having different colored eyes when he was growing up?

Gage sighed, turning down a street lined with really

nice, but older mid-century style homes. I was shocked his brother lived here. Maybe he was married.

"Having one eye that's half blue, half brown has always made me feel like a freak. Like something went wrong in the womb and made me defective." Pulling into a drive way, he put the Jeep into park before turning to me. "Don't mention anything around Tate. He—"

The front door opened and then slammed shut with a Gage lookalike striding toward us. With his glasses, he really did look like Clark Kent. He was hot, but not as hot as Gage and his tattoos.

"Don't say anything." His eyes implored me not to mention how he felt to his brother.

"I won't. I promise." I said quietly enough for only Gage to hear.

"Hop in the back, bro. Claire can't move… easily."

With both my legs jacked up, I was worried about getting up the stairs at my apartment building, but I'd deal with that once I got there.

Tate jumped in the back and clipped his seatbelt into place. "Tate this is Claire. Claire this is my little brother, Tate."

Tate rolled his eyes but leaned forward and held his hand out to shake. Turning as best as I could, I shook his hand and watched as he took me in.

"It's nice to meet you. I wish it was under better

circumstances," he indicated my broken arm. I knew my face was scratched and bruised, and the stitches on my forehead were easily visible unless I cut my bangs or wanted to have my hair pulled in front of my face. "Gage told me you were in a bad accident yesterday. I'm surprised you're out of the hospital so quickly."

"Me too, but I didn't want to stay any longer than I had to. One night is going to cost a fortune as to is."

Tate tilted his head. "No insurance?"

"I have insurance but it's shitty with a high deductible."

Gage grunted beside me but otherwise stayed quiet.

Not wanting to talk about insurance, I watched the scenery pass by in silence. Neither Gage nor Tate spoke as we made our way to the police station. Every so often I'd look over to Gage to see him eyeing his brother through the rear-view mirror. If my body hadn't been sore, I would have turned to look at Tate to see if he was looking at his brother or something else. I only hoped he wasn't looking at me.

Finding a parking place next to some white sports car, Gage put the Jeep in park before turning around with his hand on the back of my seat to look at Tate. "I'm sorry I fell asleep on you last night if you want to go over… stuff just give me a call."

I wondered what kind of stuff he was talking about,

but I knew it wasn't my place to ask no matter how curious I was.

"Will do, but I think you'll be busy for a while," Tate answered cryptically.

Did they always talk like this or was it because I was in the car?

"I've always got time for you; you just have to ask."

"Same. Now keys," Tate demanded, holding one hand out as he placed the other on my shoulder. "Claire, it was nice meeting you. I hope the next time we meet you're feeling better."

"Thanks. It was nice meeting you too." I smiled at him until I noticed Gage watching us with a frown.

Tate jumped out of the Jeep and disappeared inside the station. I'd always been nervous around cops especially when I was pulled over since I knew talking on the phone was a no-no without Bluetooth, but I couldn't afford it nor could I afford a ticket. It was strange to feel differently sitting outside the police station and with Gage and his brother. Instead I felt safe.

"Let me help you get down," Gage jumped down making me envious of his agility when I could barely move without pain shooting down my arm or one of my legs. I never knew how many muscles I used for such simple movements until every shift of my body ached.

I tried not to grimace as he helped me down. Going by the look on his face, I was unsuccessful. Imagine my surprise when Gage stopped on the other side of the white sports car and held the door open. I eyed the low seat and prepared for more pain while getting in.

Gage helped me put on my seatbelt and closed my door before running around to the driver's side. "Damn I'm sorry. I keep putting you in the worst vehicles possible with you injured."

"It's not your fault. I'm just grateful for a ride."

Gage stared at me for a long moment until I couldn't take the scrutiny any longer and looked away. "Where do you live?"

Looking back, I answered. "The Vera Cruz apartments. Do you know where that is?"

"Oh, I know where that is," his jaw ticked. "Do know how many calls we get called out to your building every week?"

"Zero?" I asked hopeful. I knew I didn't live in the best part of town, but I lived in the best place I could afford.

"More like five to ten. You need to find a new place," he growled.

Starting his car, he backed out and took a left out of the parking lot with one hand on the gear shift. I couldn't help but watch as his muscles flexed, and tattoos moved with each shift. Never before had something so simple been so hot, but everything Gage did was hot. Even the tick of his jaw.

Lost in all things Gage, I hadn't noticed we pulled up outside of my apartment building until I followed his hand to the steering wheel, and he drummed is fingers. "Where to now?"

Looking up I saw we were already there and was disappointed our time was over. "Down two more," I answered. Seeing a group of boys standing by my stairwell, I wondered how many times the cops had been called on them. Tate swore as he pulled up in front of them and parked.

"Do they normally loiter outside your building like this?" His deep voice rumbled around the inside of the car.

"Um… not normally."

"What apartment do you live in?"

"Five twenty."

His eyes narrowed as he looked up at my building. "Is there an elevator?"

"There is," I answered and watched his shoulders relax. Reaching for the door handle, I continued. "But it hasn't worked since I moved in."

"Oh, hell no." He reached over and closed the door, I'd just opened. "Do you have any place else to stay?"

Swinging my head around to look at him, I

narrowed my eyes. I appreciated his help, but he wasn't going to make me feel like shit about where I lived.

"No, I don't have any place else to stay nor can I afford one." And here I thought he was a good guy until he made me feel like shit for being poor. "Thank you for driving me home, but I think our time ends here."

Before I could open my door again, Gage was peeling out of the parking lot.

5

———

GAGE

"Are you kidnapping me?"

"Hardly and even if I was what are you going to do about it? Call the police on me?" I laughed at the thought of what the guys would think if they got a call saying I'd kidnapped some sweet, beautiful woman.

"What the hell do you think you're doing then?" Claire glared at me from the other side of the car.

"I am not letting you stay here while you can barely move and those…" Thugs came to mind, but I wasn't going to say it. I had a feeling she wouldn't appreciate what I thought of her neighbors. "Those men out there—"

"Don't you dare finish that sentence," Claire seethed. I could feel the venom dripping from her words all the way over here. "I've never had a problem in the six months I've lived here." She huffed and her hair went flying. I bit the inside of my cheek to keep from grinning. It was cute as fuck and I didn't want to piss her off more than I already had. In truth, I had no idea what the hell I was doing. I hadn't been interested in a woman in I didn't know how long. Maybe ever. And I was about to do something most definitely stupid.

Keeping my tone light, I tried to explain why. "While I'm happy you haven't had any problems in the six months you've been here. I've been here a hell of a lot longer than you and I know the crime rate in that area and how many calls we get sent out to your build-ing." If I had to, I would scare her with the stats of what all goes down in the place she calls home if it would make her see reason. It wasn't like she was going to be able to get up and down those stairs unless someone carried her, or she wanted it to take a couple of hours anyway. "Look I've got an apartment on the first floor (which I hated until this moment) that I'm barely us. You can stay there until you can move around better. In fact, for the next six days, I'll be working the night shift so while I'm up you'll be asleep and vice versa."

"Is this some type of trick? Are you a serial killer or something?" Her bitter laugh filled the interior of my car.

My blood chilled at her mention of a serial killer.

After talking to Tate last night, it looked as if Oasis had a serial killer in its midst and that was nothing to laugh about.

"Hey," she placed her hand on my arm. Her body in an awkward position because of her cast and injuries. "I was kidding. Kind of. I mean I know I got attached to you last night and all, but you're not responsible for me, and you most definitely don't have to do this."

"I wouldn't offer if I didn't want to. Like I said, I'm barely home and if it would make you feel better, I can stay with my brother."

"No... I... I will not kick you out of your house, Gage. Are you sure you want to do this? I'm a stranger." Her voice was quiet and nervous.

You're more than a stranger.

Claire gasped from beside me.

Had I said that out loud?

"Do you... do you feel the same connection I feel?" She bit her bottom lip as her eyes shined with hope.

Was that what this was? A strange connection.

My grip on the steering wheel tightened as I sped up. Why did she make me want to open up to her?

"I feel something, but I'm not sure what it is." Claire's shoulders slumped and I wanted to kick my own ass for disappointing her. "I didn't mean it like that. It's... I'm not sure how to describe it because I've never felt this way before, but I wouldn't paint it nega-tively. It feels… hopeful. Good."

Fuck why was I telling her all of this? I could have just said yes and been done with it. Instead she had me spilling my guts like some teenage girl.

Claire beamed from the passenger side of my car while I wanted to sew my mouth closed so I didn't say too much. I mean really what was I doing? Claire was just barely getting started in life at twenty-four years old and I had an established career on the police force. To top it all off, I was eleven years older than her. I didn't see how anything could work between us.

We pulled up in front of my apartment in silence. I was lucky my neighbors always left the parking place right in front of my apartment empty. I had a feeling they did it because I'm a cop and they wanted to kiss up to me. I appreciated it. I didn't want Claire to have to walk any further than she had to. She had to be incredibly sore.

I helped her out of the car and ushered her into my apartment surprised she hadn't argued more about staying with me. But really what choice did she have unless she really did call the police. Although I'd like to think they wouldn't believe I'd do something like kidnap a young girl.

I watch as Claire looks around my apartment. It's what you'd expect a thirty-five-year-old bachelor to live like. One big ass leather couch that took up most of the living room. A matching recliner and a TV that spanded the length of one wall.

She spinned around slowly taking it all in. I was happy there wasn't beer bottles and pizza boxes littered on every surface. The maid had been by sometime between when I left yesterday and now. Finally, she sat down on one end of my couch before she faced me. "Is your brother married?"

"Uh," I chuckled since Tate never had a girlfriend so there was no opportunity for him to get married. "Quite the opposite." He's more like a monk. "Why?"

She shrugged as a blush crept up her cheeks. "Your places are quite opposite to use your words against you."

"Oh, you mean because he lives in a nice house and I live in a tiny apartment?"

"Your apartment is nice, but I don't think most men own houses unless they're at least in a committed relationship," she blushed again. This time it spread down to her chest and I had to walk into the kitchen to resist my urge to see how far it went down her body and will away my semi-erect cock.

"Do you want anything to drink?" I checked my refrigerator to see I only had beer and water. Shit I'd need to make a trip to the store if she was staying here. "I've got beer and water."

"I'll take a water if it's not too much trouble," she called.

Pulling out two waters, I made my way back to her. My dick under control. "Guys your age don't normally have houses unless they're married or in a relationship," I handed her, her water. "But it's more common for guys my age or so Tate tells me." I chuckled to myself. Tate was always trying to get me to buy a house telling me what a good investment it was.

Claire tilted her head and eyed me up and down. "How old are you?"

"Thirty-five."

Her big gray eyes widened. "There's no way you're in your thirties."

"I can show you my license if you don't believe me." I pulled out my wallet.

"I believe you, but damn you don't look a day over twenty-eight. Max. If I had to guess I'd say..." she tilted her head from side to side while chewing her bottom lip. Damn if I didn't want to take it between my teeth and nibble on it as well. "Twenty-six."

It was nice to hear I didn't look over a decade older than her. Maybe people wouldn't wonder what she was doing with someone so much older than her when they saw us out. I shook my head trying to eliminate the thoughts of us together. Where was this coming from?

Then why was she here in your apartment if you don't want to be with her?

"Nice. Next time you see Tate tell him he looks forty," I leaned over laughing. Tate would burst a vessel if Claire told him he looked so old.

"Oh no, I'm not going to lie to him. I won't be a part of your games and make him not like me," she giggled and then winced. "Would you mind if I took some of my pain meds and took a little nap? They make my head all foggy and tired."

Fuck, I should have taken her there first thing. If I wasn't thinking with my dick, I would have noticed the pain reflecting in her eyes.

"Sure. Let me show you to the guest bedroom. I should have taken you first thing."

"Do you have a t-shirt I could borrow?" She looked up at me with a frown. "I don't have anything else to wear," she pulled at the hem of the scrubs the hospital had given her.

"I'm sorry, Claire. I wasn't thinking when—"

"When you took off like a bat out of hell from my apartment building?" She smiled at me like all was forgiven.

"Yeah, you'll probably want some clothes to wear while you're here. If you give me your key and a list, I can pick up your stuff for you on my way home from work."

"Oh, I guess," she looked down and picked at her shirt.

Was she embarrassed? Did she not want me to see where she lived?

"Or we could go tomorrow afternoon before I have to go to work. Would that work? Maybe you'll be feeling a little better then and it will be easier for you to get up the stairs."

I had a feeling her elevator hadn't worked in a very long time. Kind of like the one on The Big Bang Theory.

"Maybe."

"In the meantime, you can borrow one of my t-shirts."

"Thanks," she meekly answered.

I wasn't sure why there was a shift in her mood. Maybe it was because she was tired and in pain. Whatever the reason I'd give her some space after I got her something of mine to wear.

6

GAGE

FOR THE LAST WEEK, I'D SPENT AS LITTLE TIME AS possible at my apartment. With Claire there wearing my favorite t-shirt I'd given her to wear to bed and the vanilla lotion she wore it was everything I could do not to rip off her clothes and throw her down. To keep temptation at bay, I slept during the day and I worked as much as possible.

Each day Claire moved around a little easier and this afternoon when I came out of my bedroom ready for work, she was walking to the living room without a limp. When I met her face on, I looked down to find her knee was no longer swollen and had moved from a dark purple bruise to a light green one.

Now as I drove home tired as fuck from working the night shift and all the overtime, all I could think about is Claire and what she'd look like spread out beneath me. It's been a recurring dream every night she's been staying with me and been on a constant loop in my mind while working. More than once at work I've had to arrange my dick so no one can see the tent in my pants. She's been driving me mad no matter how hard I've tried to keep my distance, but I was done with that. Tonight, I was going to make her dinner and see where this was going.

Walking into my apartment, I looked around in the pitch-dark living room. Not a light was on, not a sound was heard, and I started to get worried. I was home early by a few hours, so it wasn't late.

"Claire," I called out, making my way down the hall toward the bedrooms. Again, it was completely dark. Had she left without telling me? Knocking on the guest room door, I placed my ear to the door and listened. I heard a light groan and wanted to kick down the door. Luckily when I tried the knob the door was unlocked. Pushing the door open, I flicked on the light to find Claire on the bed with her body tangled up in the sheets and a pillow wrapped around her head.

"Turn off the light," she groaned pulling the pillow tighter around her head, her entire body tense.

Flipping the light off, I made my way over to the bed and sat on the edge where she was now curved into a ball. Placing my hand on her shoulder, I asked with my brows furrowed as I tried to see her under the pillow. "Claire, are you okay?"

"Please talk quieter?" She croaked out then stiffened.

I lowered my voice. "What's wrong?"

"My head." Her body tensed and then her legs curled around my back.

"Do you have a headache?" I whispered, lifting the pillow off her head.

Her forehead and face were marred in pain. Her brows were drawn with her lips pulled down in a frown.

"It's the worst headache of my life."

The only light was coming from the window and the sun had started to set. My eyes had finally adjusted to the dim light when a lone tear slipped down her cheek.

I stood from the bed. "I'll go get you some ibuprofen."

Her hand wrapped around my wrist, stopping me. "I've been taking it all day and my headache has only gotten worse. I can't take anymore."

Concerned I asked quietly. "Do you normally get headaches like this?"

"Never." Her lip trembled as she squeezed her eyes shut.

Taking her hand in mine, I lightly squeezed. I didn't want to do anything that would make her headache worse. It seemed like a migraine to me. I didn't get them, but Tate did. There were a few times he had to go to the ER and get a shot of something to finally make his go away. Maybe I needed to take her to the hospital and have her checked out.

"I think you have a migraine and I should probably take you to the hospital if it has only gotten worse with you taking ibuprofen."

Claire shook her head and then clutched her head. Her body started to tremble which scared the shit out of me. "Please no. I can't afford another hospital visit. If it's still bad tomorrow, I'll go to urgent care."

I wasn't sure urgent care would have what she'd need, but I wasn't going to argue with her and make things worse.

"How about I call Tate? He gets migraines sometimes and I bet if I explained the situation to him, he'd give you whatever he takes when he has one."

"Do you really think he'd do that?" The hope in her delicate voice had me pulling out my phone to call my brother. I hated seeing her in pain and if I could do something to make it better I would.

"I think he would. I'll be right back. I'm going to give him a call." I stood just outside her bedroom door as I made the call to my brother. When it rang for the fourth time, I was worried he wasn't going to answer. For all I knew he could have been out on a case.

"Detective Walker," he answered on the fifth ring. He was most definitely busy if he hadn't looked at his caller ID to see who was calling.

"Baby bro, are you busy?" I whispered.

"I am," his voice went from stiff to concerned. "Why are you whispering?"

"Because I came home to find Claire laying down in the dark with a horrible headache. I think it's a migraine and she refuse to go to the hospital so I was hoping you could give her what you take when your headaches get bad." I relayed him with everything in one breath.

"Does she normally get headaches?"

"She says she doesn't."

"I don't exactly feel comfortable giving her some of my medicine in case it's something else. It seems a little late for it to have something to do with her wreck, but it could be. What if she has a brain bleed?"

Dramatic much?

"I don't think it matters what I say to her she'll refuse to go to the hospital." I hated that she felt she couldn't go because she was so worried about how much it would cost her. In reality I knew that was the case for many people, but I still hated to see it. "What if I promise to keep an eye on her and I take her tomorrow if she's not any better or still has symptoms?"

Tate sighed and I knew he was running his fingers

through his hair. "Fine. I'll have to run home to grab it, but I'll try to be fast. "

"Thanks bro. I hate seeing her like this. I've always hated seeing you when you had a migraine and I was helpless to do anything to make you better."

"I know," he grunted. "I'll be over as soon as I can. Until then make the room as dark as possible and keep the environment cool and quiet."

"Got it." I headed directly for the window and closed the blinds, so no light came in. "See you soon," I murmured into the phone.

"Gage," Claire moaned out my name.

Sitting down beside her on the bed, I ran my fingers through her hair. The moment I touched her; Claire's body relaxed. "I'm here. Tate's going to bring you something to make you feel better."

"I don't feel good." She whimpered, clutching onto one of my hands.

"I know. Hopefully you'll feel better soon."

With my free hand, my fingers started to massage her head and down her neck. Even her scalp was tense, but as the minutes went by the tension slowly started to ease. She was close to sleep when Tate lightly tapped on the bedroom door. I waved him in not wanting to interrupt her by standing. I could feel his eyes assessing us as he strode forward with a pill bottle in his hand.

"Any better?" His voice was soft and smooth, but I

could feel the tension radiating off him. I wasn't sure why, but I couldn't question him at the moment with Claire lying next to me in physical pain.

"A little. I think. I was massaging her neck and scalp, and she slowly started to relax. I think she was almost asleep."

"I'll leave a couple of pills here, but maybe wait to see if first she can sleep. Maybe that will help."

I stood from the bed as gently as I could and pulled Tate out of the room with me. Once we were in the living room, I wheeled around on him and hissed. "What's your problem? If you didn't want to give her your drugs you could have saved us both the trouble and told me over the phone."

His eyes narrowed, but he kept his voice low. "*I* don't have a problem, but this isn't you Gage. From the moment you mentioned her to me, you've been different."

"So what? Why not be happy for me? Maybe I found someone."

Tate wrapped one arm around my shoulder. "I just don't want you to get hurt."

"Why do you think I'll get hurt?" I cupped my hand over his shoulder and squeezed.

"I don't know how to explain it, but I've got a feeling in the pit of my stomach she's going to hurt you.

I'll I can say is be careful." His face softened. "You know I love you, bro."

"I feel it," I patted my chest over my heart.

"Me too. Always." Tate placed his hand over his heart. It was something we'd done since we were little kids.

Letting out a deep breath, I tried to explain what I was feeling. "I was planning on making her dinner and seeing where this was going tonight, and I came home to this. I've tried to stay away, but I can't stop thinking about her no matter how hard I try. I've never felt like this before and I thought… I don't know what to think. Somehow in those few minutes at the wreck site she worked her way under my skin."

"I know and that's what scares me."

"What do I do?" I hung my head while my shoulders slumped.

Tate let out a deep sigh and placed his hand back on my shoulder. "Hell, if I know. Do what feels right. I only want you happy."

"I know you do. I want you happy too."

I looked up to see Tate shaking his head. I didn't understand why he seemed determined to be miserable and alone. If only he'd talk to me maybe I could understand what went on in his head.

Wrapping his hand around the door knob, he looked back at me over his shoulder. "Look I've got to go. Let her sleep and then give her a pill if she needs it. If she takes one and isn't better by tomorrow night you have to take her to the ER even if she doesn't want to. Even if she says she can't afford it."

"I know." I was already going against what I knew I should for this girl. "Thanks for doing this. I know you're busy."

"You don't have to thank me. You know I'll always do anything for you. I'll talk to you soon."

"Soon," I gave him a chin lift and went back to Claire.

7

GAGE

Sitting at the kitchen island, I sipped on my third cup of coffee as I read through my emails on my phone. I hardly slept last night in the guest room chair. Every time I nodded off to sleep, I'd wake up and check on Claire to make sure she was okay. She woke up whimpering about the pain in her head about an hour after Tate left, but once she took one of his pills, she settled down pretty quickly and slept the rest of the night. Too bad I wasn't so lucky.

How had this little redheaded woman with eyes the color of a spring storm wrapped me around her little finger in such a short time I had no idea?

"Hey," Claire's voice croaked as she walked into the living room. My apartment was an open floor plan with the living room leading into the kitchen. "Thanks for taking care of me last night. I'm not sure what I would have done without your brother's pill."

I dipped my chin and yawned as I took her in. Her long red hair was a rat's nest that trailed down her back, but her eyes sparkled with life. She still wore the t-shirt I gave her to wear every night to bed and still had it on now. It fell down to mid-thigh and showed her creamy long legs tempting me more than anyone dressed in the finest or skimpiest of clothing. "Are you feeling any better?"

"Oh gosh," Claire held her hand to her head. "What a difference a day makes. Literally, I guess huh." She motioned at the kitchen window where the sun was shining through. "I'm so glad I'm feeling better this morning. I almost let you take me to the hospital it was so unbearable. It's not right for someone to be in that much pain."

"No, it isn't."

I wanted to ask about her insurance, but I didn't. I knew deductibles on most plans were high and people paid and arm and a leg for their insurance. I heard about it almost daily from calls I went out on.

"Sorry, I'm rambling. It feels strange to see you sitting here just drinking coffee being… normal. You're usually up and out." She fisted the hem of her shirt and twisted it. I tried to keep my eyes off her legs and how high her shirt was moving up with each twist. "I kind of feel like you've been avoiding me."

"I haven't." I lied.

"I know you said you had to work the night shift and all, but…" She shrugged and hung her head. "I didn't realize I wouldn't be seeing you at *all*. It's weird staying at a strangers house let alone being all by myself most of the time." Her mouth thinned out into a line. "Even if it is you."

"Hey, look at me." Claire lifted her head and locked eyes with me. "I'm sorry I left you alone so much this week. I feel bad about it and I planned to make you dinner last night as an apology."

"Really?" Her voice pitched high. Her entire face changed as her eyes lit up and sparkled, her posture straightened, and she bounced in place.

"Really." A grin stretched across my face. "Do you like Chicken Parmesan?"

"Yes, I love it. I love anything Italian." she clapped her hands together. "Is that what you were going to make?" Her voice switched to soft and sweet just like her.

My grin grew until her stomach rumbled and I could hear it from all the way across the room, and it instantly fell away. Standing I went to the refrigerator and looked inside. "Did you eat anything yesterday?"

"Um… I don't think so. I was going to make some breakfast when my headache started. It came on fast and then I was nauseous for most of the day." She closed her eyes and took in a deep breath.

I rushed over to her with a bottle of water in my hand. "Are you okay? Is it coming back?"

"No, I'm just hungry. Starving. I could eat everything in this kitchen." Her stomach grumbled again.

"Let me make you some eggs and bacon. While you wait throw some bread in the toaster to nibble on."

I set about making us some breakfast by putting eggs and bacon in two pans. I didn't normally eat it instead I usually had coffee, but I'd make the exception for her so she wouldn't be uncomfortable while I sat and stared at her while she ate.

Claire pulled the toaster out and filled it up with bread before leaning against the counter and watching me. "Where'd you learn to cook?"

Adding cheese to the eggs, I stirred it all together. "Mostly myself. When I was young sometimes, I'd watch my mom make dinner or whatever, but unfortunately for me it's mostly been experimenting with what I like to eat."

"You could eat out or have a girlfriend make it." The last was said so quietly I had to glance out of the side of my eye to see what her game was. Was Claire trying to get me to confess to having a girlfriend?

"When Tate and I first moved here I didn't always have the money to eat out that's why I taught myself. As for a girlfriend to make me food," I cleared my throat at what I was about to confess. "I've never really had a girlfriend per se to cook for me."

Claire jumped up on the counter and swung her legs. "I find that hard to believe. You've got a lot of things working for you."

"Really? What kind of things?" I turned to see her cheeks had pinked up and I grinned to myself.

"Do you really need me to tell you? I wouldn't think you'd need an ego boost."

"I think I do since I haven't had a girlfriend."

"I think that's more of your doing than the women, but I'll tell you since you're making me food." Her legs stopped and she clasped her hands together. "One you're incredibly good looking. Anyone would die to date a man who looked like you. Second, add the tattoos and you've got the bad boy thing down pat."

My body tensed. I wasn't bad per se, but I wasn't always a boy scout. "Do you think I'm a bad boy?"

"In all honesty. No, but you look like one. Women love a bad boy or a man who looks bad but is secretly a softy."

I was most definitely not a softy.

Maybe I was for Claire, my mother and brother, but that was it.

"Is that it?"

She rolled her eyes at me but smiled. "No, third as if you didn't have enough working in your favor, women love a man in uniform."

From my experience women loved looking at men in uniform but didn't love the danger that uniform put them in on a daily basis. It took a strong woman to be with a man who was in the line of duty. I knew it was all my fault I hadn't had a serious girlfriend, but it made me realize I had no right to give Tate a hard time.

I turned back to the stove and finished making our breakfast while she ate a piece of toast and eyed me the whole time. Sitting down our plates full of food on the island, I stood on the opposite side while Claire sat on a bar stool while we ate.

"This is good. I've never put cheese in my eggs, and I was a little worried."

A low chuckle escaped as I bit into a piece of bacon. "You should have said something."

"Then I'd be missing out." She chewed on her scrambled eggs. Tilting her head to the side, she asked. "When do you have to be at work?"

"Tuesday afternoon."

That gave us two days for us to get to know each other better. Hopefully without our clothes on.

"Have you talked to your job?" My brows furrowed realizing I had no idea what she did. "What do you do exactly? I don't think I've ever asked."

"I'm an ASL interpreter. Mostly at concerts and events."

Definitely not what I was expecting. I leaned my hip into the counter and picked up a piece of bacon. "That's really cool. How'd you get into sign language?"

"My dad," she smiled as her eyes lit up. "He lost his hearing when he was in his twenties, so I grew up signing and interpreting for him."

"Are you close?"

"Very. He raised me all on his own," she frowned, taking a bite of eggs.

Where was her mom? Was that why she was upset now?

"My mom raised Tate and I all on her own." I stood and took my plate to the sink. With my back to her, I finished. "Our dad left when we were two months old and was never in the picture."

I didn't hear Claire as she came up behind me and placed her hand in the middle of my back. "I'm sorry, Gage. That couldn't have been easy on you or your mother."

Turning back to her, I placed my hands on her tiny waist grounding myself. "It wasn't. We put our mom through some serious hell growing up. I can't imagine raising two boys like us while working enough to support us. We were always getting into something, but I think that's the price of living in a small town. With nothing to occupy your time, you find plenty of things to do you shouldn't and become your parent's worst nightmare. Or that's how our mom made it sound."

Her hands came to rest on top of my arms. "What kind of trouble?"

"Drinking, stealing her car, fighting. You name it we probably did it." It was surprising we were both cops with how we started out.

"What made you stop?" She looked up at me through her long lashes. Her gray eyes implored me to tell her all my secrets.

Dropping my arms, I took a step back but ran into the counter. Crossing my arms over my chest, I leaned back. "Tate and I were out causing mischief, and someone broke into our house while our mom was there. It was a wakeup call for both of us. A cop lived a couple of houses down and was driving by at the right time to come home. He went to check out why our door was open in the middle of the night. He found the perp pointing a gun at my mom." It was hard to swallow thinking about that night. I hated thinking about all the what ifs that could have happened if he hadn't been driving by or hadn't come over. Would the intruder have killed my mom?

Claire stepped closer, placing her hand on my chest all the while never breaking eye contact. "She's okay and now you and your brother are out there helping others just like that cop did for your mom" Her lips tipped up as if she liked the idea of us out there helping people. "I find that very admirable, Gage. Thank you for sharing that story with me. I know it wasn't easy."

It wasn't easy but once again I spilled my guts to her when I didn't want to. I certainly didn't feel admirable. For months our mom woke up having nightmares about that night and all we could do was go in there and try to calm her down until she could go back to sleep. If we hadn't been out that night, she wouldn't have left the front door unlocked and wouldn't have been waiting up in the kitchen to make sure we got home safe. We had made her unsafe by being stupid.

Her other hand cupped my cheek. "It's not your fault," Claire whispered.

It sure as fuck felt like it. Even after all these years, I still felt the guilt. The guilt that ate away at me was why I didn't call or visit my mom as much as I should.

Pulling away, I headed to my room. I needed to be by myself for a little while. "I'm going to take a shower. Finish eating your breakfast and I'll clean up later," I called without looking back.

"Sure," she said not hiding the disappointment in her tone.

I was disappointed in my teenage self and my adult self. I needed to be a better son and not let the guilt plaguing me keep me from my mom. It seemed right that I would disappoint Claire too. I couldn't help it. It was a pattern I was all too good at.

8

CLAIRE

I STOOD STUNNED. WHAT THE HELL JUST HAPPENED? One minute I thought Gage was going to kiss me and the next he was a totally different man. A man with demons eating at him since he was a teenager. It made me wonder if his brother knew or if he felt the same guilt.

Instead of waiting for Gage to come back and clean up breakfast like he said he would, I filled the sink with water and started washing. I needed something to do beside stand where he left me wondering what I'd done wrong. It was only right since he'd made breakfast and let me stay here for the last week. I was thinking now that I could move around better it was time for me to go home and I had a feeling I'd overstayed my welcome. With my broken arm, I wasn't sure how much I could work with the limited mobility in my hand so I'd probably have to either find a new apartment that I could afford in an even worse part of town or find a roommate. I wasn't too excited about either of those prospects, but it was better than being homeless. In the short amount of time I'd lived in California I'd found living here wasn't cheap.

"I told you I'd do that when I was done." Gage rumbled behind me making me jump and splash soap suds all over the front of me.

Twirling around with my hand over my heart, I narrowed my eyes at him. "Give a girl some warning. You nearly gave me a heart attack."

A faint grin twitched on his lips, but otherwise he stared down at me. After a few moments, I started to feel uneasy when his eyes never moved from my t-shirt. Looking down I flushed red. With the shirt wet, it was completely see-through, and my stiff nipples were on display and showing Gage how attracted to him I really was. There was no hiding it. Crossing my arms over my chest, I scowled at Gage. "I'm going to go change. After that I think it might be best if you took me home."

"Shit Claire, I'm sorry. I didn't mean to scare you and as for seeing your boobs, I'm a warm-blooded male. I couldn't help it." He shrugged like because he was of the male species it gave him the right to look at my breasts when I had no idea, I was flashing him. "I was transfixed. They're perfect. I've been dreaming of them since we met, and my imagination didn't do them justice."

I'd never been told my boobs were perfect and to have Gage tell me definitely helped soothe my ego. I was sure even though he said he'd never had a girl-friend; he'd seen plenty of women's breasts. I wouldn't be surprised if he didn't have at least one woman a day throwing themselves at him. He was gorgeous with a chiseled face and a strong defined jawline, I wanted to lick and nibble. The tattoos that covered his arms gave him the air of a bad boy, but deep down I had a feeling he really was a softy. His multi-color eyes were the most incredible thing I'd ever seen. I'd never met anyone with two different colored eyes, but one of the actors on one of my favorite TV shows, Shadowhunter's had heterochromia. After seeing him on screen, I had to look up his eyes otherwise I'd never know what it was called. It was more incredible in person. Gage may have felt like a freak because of his eyes, but I thought it set him apart and made him even more alluring.

"Do you really have to go home?" He asked breaking me out of my musings about him and his body.

Shaking my head, I smiled up at him. "I think so. I'm almost at a hundred percent and I don't want to overstay my welcome."

"You're not and I'm sorry if I've made you feel that

way." He looked up at the ceiling and took a deep breath before looking down and locking eyes on me. "Can you stay a couple more days? Until I have to go back to work so we can get to know each other better?"

I was shocked he wanted me to stay. I definitely wouldn't be opposed to it. If I was lucky, I'd get to see him without his shirt on and if I was really lucky, I'd get to see Gage with nothing on at all.

He took a step closer until there was only an inch separating us. If I swayed even the slightest, my breasts would graze his chest. "What do you say? I'll make you dinner and everything."

"*Everything?*" I quirked up one eyebrow.

His grin grew salacious, his strong arms wrapped around my waist and pulled me flush against his hard body. "Anything you want."

"Deal." I placed my hands on his firm chest and raised up on my tippy-toes to kiss him. Gage didn't make me wait. He swooped down, slanting his mouth over mine, and took me in a dizzying kiss. His lips were soft but demanding as his tongue worked its way to brush against mine. I felt a low groan vibrate and work its way up from his belly and into my mouth, making my core pulse with want. No man had ever wanted me as much as Gage and knowing I affected him like he did me was a heady aphrodisiac.

My arms wrapped around his neck and held on.

One of his hands disappeared under the t-shirt I'd been wearing to bed all week and skimmed up my back and then back down. His fingertips dipped into my panties and cupped my ass cheeks, squeezing hard as he lifted me on top of his counter.

Warm calloused fingers skated up my outer thighs as Gage nudged my legs open and moved in between them. Both hands went to the hem of my shirt and pulled it over my head, leaving me in only my white thong. One hand went to the back of my head and the other to my chest as he pressed me down until I was laid out on the counter. My back arched off the cool countertop and bowed even more as Gage took one breast in his mouth and the other with his hand. His warm tongue swirled around my nipple; lust heated every ounce of my blood.

"You taste even better than I imagined." His mouth traveled south and nipped at my belly. One lone finger hooked into the wet fabric of my thong and pulled the material down my legs. Bringing his hands back up, Gage spread my legs wide, his thumb skimmed through my folds as his eyes turned dark and stormy. "Fucking hell, Claire. I never expected you to be bare." Eyes never leaving my pussy, he dipped down, his long tongue swiping through my lips.

We both moaned at the same time. One lick and I never wanted him to leave from the space between my legs. With his face buried between my thighs, he murmured sending delicious vibrations through my core. "Every inch of you I taste gets better and better. I'm going to feast on your pussy until the end of time. Worship you day and night."

Gage didn't disappoint. He spent the better part of an hour with using his tongue and fingers to bring me over the edge over and over again until I was literally seeing stars. My body was splayed over the counter without a care in the world. Every few seconds my leg would twitch with after effects from all the orgasms Gage had given me.

I watched as he stood to his full height, stretching his head from side to side. A wide grin graced his face, eye sparkling. Ripping a condom packet open, he sheathed his thick cock. My breath caught at the size of him. I wasn't sure what I was expecting, but it wasn't what was in front of me now. I swallowed roughly as he stepped toward me. Hands on my hips, Gage pulled me to the edge of the counter and ran the tip of his cock through my drenched pussy. His deep voice was full of gravel as he spoke. "Are you ready for me?"

Even exhausted, I was desperate to have his thick length fill and stretch me beyond anything I'd ever experienced in my life. I licked my lips and nodded. I wasn't sure I could speak even if I tried. My voice had grown hoarse after crying out Gage's name repeatedly.

Pulling me gently off the counter, Gage turned me around like I was a rag doll and pushed me to bend over the counter. Spreading my legs, he lined up at my entrance and pushed in with one thrust. Gage folded himself around me, molding his back to mine. One hand grasped my hip as he held still letting me get accustomed to his size. My walls stretched and clenched around his massive length. Slowly he started to move inside me pulling almost all the way out until the tip of his cock rimmed my entrance and then moving back inside just as slowly. I gripped the other side of the counter and started to push back with every stroke.

Gage lifted himself up, his hands spread my ass cheeks as he watched his cock move in and out of me. "You feel fan-fucking-tastic. Arch your ass up higher for me."

I lifted my ass as Gage moved back inside of me, he hit a spot in me no one had ever touched. I curved my ass up higher almost coming on the spot as Gage hit that sweet spot. "Oh my God, Gage, keep doing whatever you're doing." I begged.

His thrusts quickened and his grip on my hips tightened as he kissed up my spine. He was rough yet gentle. He was everything in that moment and I never wanted it to stop. Turning my head, our mouths crashed together. Our tongues dueled feverishly matching the pace of our thrusts. Tingles traveled down my spine.

My toes curled as my walls clenched around his hot length.

Gage groaned in my ear and pumped once more before stilling inside me. I felt his cock pulse in time with my walls milking him as he came inside of me. Resting his front to my back, Gage panted into my neck. His hands glided down my arms, tickling my overheated skin. Our fingers laced together, and we exhaled.

Picking me up bridal style, Gage walked us to his couch. He handled me as if I was light as a feather laying down and then draping me on top of him. Strong arms wrapped around me, holding me tight to his sweaty muscular body. Being in Gage's arms felt like home. A home I wasn't going to be ready to leave in a couple of days.

9

GAGE

WE SPENT THE NEXT TWO DAYS UNTIL I HAD TO GO back to work in bed barely coming up for air. I cooked her the dinner I had promised since we both needed our strength. If I thought I was in trouble by constantly thinking of her before, I was now completely under Claire's spell. I couldn't get enough of her. Everything about her was perfect. She was sweet, smart and fun, and better yet me being a cop didn't seem to faze her one ounce. She was so perfect I was desperate to see her after working the last two days. I took Claire home before I had to go back to work and hadn't seen her since. We'd talked briefly, but it wasn't enough for me. I wanted to touch her, to gaze upon her lush curves, and run my hands all over her body. Tonight, I was taking her on our first official date, and I couldn't wait. First, I had to run into the station and talked to my brother before running home to take a quick shower and change.

I rounded the corner and saw Tate at his desk with his head down reading over something. We hadn't talked much since he'd brought over the pills for Claire, but I didn't take it personally. Hell, he was trying to track down a serial killer so chatting with me was not a top priority. I sat down in a chair in front of his desk and crossed one foot over my other leg's knee and waited to see how long it would take him to realize I was there.

Five minutes later, Tate's eyes met mine before going wide. He sat back in his chair, pulled his glasses off, and rubbed at his bloodshot eyes. A low chuckle emanated from him. "How long have you been sitting there staring at me?"

Glancing down at my right arm, I checked my watch and tapped its face. "Right around five minutes. I didn't want to bother you."

He blew out a frustrated breath. "We'd be here until the end of time if you were waiting on me. Fuck Gage, we have no leads. Not. A. One. I don't want another person to have to die and for this guy to make a mistake for us to figure out who it is." Leaning forward, he rested his face in his hands.

I had a bad feeling there was more. I knew he was frustrated about this guy who liked to kill red heads.

"There's something else besides this guy isn't there? Have you given him a name yet or has the press?"

"Not yet. We haven't given out too many details so it should be difficult to conceptualize it's the same killer."

"Are you sure it's the same guy?" I knew he was but just maybe it was a fluke and he could rest easier.

Tate straightened up and his midnight blue eyes bored into me. "Yes, I'm fucking sure. How many people are out there killing women who have red hair and scalping them? In Oasis and the surrounding towns?" He added as if he needed to clarify.

"I sure hope there isn't more than one. One is too many."

"It is." He steepled his fingers into of his lips getting ready to tell me something he knew I wouldn't like.

"Is mom okay?" I had called her after I took Claire home and promised I'd visit her soon. Maybe I'd even take Claire with me.

"Mom's fine and over the moon you called and talked to her about a girl." A wry grin started to spread across his face but stopped abruptly. "I wasn't sure if you knew or not, but I wanted to tell you just in case so you could warn Claire."

Claire?

I sat up straighter in my seat. He had my full attention. Why did he want to talk about Claire?

"Don't freak out. Not yet, but I thought you and Claire should know. There's been multiple cops' girlfriend's and wives attacked lately."

"Attacked? Where?" And what did this have to do with me and Claire?

"Yes, it's been at varies places throughout Oasis. Places they were known to be at and when they came outside, they were held at gunpoint. One was almost raped. We think she was the first one, but all the rest have been beat up. Last night Williamson's girlfriend was attacked outside Vons," Tate closed his eyes and shook his head. "She's in the hospital. From what I've heard she should be fine, but she's messed up pretty bad. Each attack keeps escalating and I think you should warn Claire to carry mace with her when she's alone and to make sure her apartment is secure."

This time it was me who leaned forward. With my elbows on my knees, I hung my head. I couldn't believe what I'd heard. Who the hell was dumb enough to attack multiple police officer's girlfriends and wives? They'd be lucky to get away with their life once caught. Maybe I should chill things out with Claire until this asshole or assholes is caught?

My head popped up to find Tate looking at me sympathetically. "Do you think it's a gang thing?"

"I don't know much about it," he shook his head. "I've got my hands full, so Allen is on the case. I'd tell you to go talk to him, but I know how much you don't like him."

I gave him my best withering look. It wasn't like Tate liked him. In fact, most of my beef with Allen is because of him being an asshole to Tate. He was constantly asking if he was fucking the Chief, who by the way was a man not some knockout, to make detective. "You don't either. He's a douchebag on his best day."

"I don't but I try to ignore him and his bullshit. You're out there on calls, but I have to deal with his ass stuck in a room too small for the two of us." He took a deep breath in and sat back. "I'll let you know if I find anything else out, but in the meantime tell Claire to be careful."

"I will. Thanks for looking out for her." I sat on the edge of my chair ready to bolt. The need to see her was greater than ever. "Is there anything else? I have a date tonight with Claire."

He looked me up and down. "No man. Go have fun. Where are you taking her?"

"Manny's."

"You must really like her to take her there." He scanned me one more time. "Are you going in your uniform?"

"No jackass. I've got to go home to shower and change first. That's why I'm in a hurry. Although I think she likes me in uniform." I waggled my eyebrows up and down as I smoothed down my shirt.

Tate pretended to gag but smiled. "Get out of here and I'll talk to you later."

I stood feeling energized at the notion I'd see Claire soon. "Later."

<hr>

"You really won't tell me where we're going?" Claire asked with a giggle.

She looked incredible tonight. Her bruising was almost gone, and her knee was no longer swollen. I knew because she was wearing short shorts that show-cased her legs. They were long and tanned, perfect to wrap around my waist. Dainty feet slid out of her flip-flops and tapped along with the radio. Her lacy tank top dipped low enough to give me a view of her perfect tits. The best part about her was her big gray eyes shining with excitement.

"You don't want me to ruin the surprise, do you?"

"I'm not good with surprises, but for you I'll try to be patient." She rested her hand on mine and flashed me a smile. I laced our fingers together as well as I could with her cast.

I grinned as her knee bounced in anticipation. My only hope was she wasn't disappointed in Manny's. We pulled up to a staggering long line, but I didn't mind with Claire on my arm. We'd be lucky to be eating in thirty minutes.

"Wow, it's busy." I could hear the skepticism in her voice. She thought it was a shit hole with its run-down sign with the 'A' light out for the last two years or so.

"I promise it's good. The best tacos in a two-hundred-mile radius. Maybe more." I jumped out of the car and made my way over to her side to help her out of the car, but Claire was already up and out. Instead I took her hand in mine. "I was going to get the door."

Claire linked her fingers with mine and smiled up at me. "That's sweet and all, but I'm tired of being an invalid. Treat me how you'd treat any date."

I couldn't remember the last date I'd been on, but that didn't matter. I'd treat Claire better than I had any of them.

As we stepped up to the back of the line, I pulled her flush against me and looked down into bright but stormy eyes. "I wasn't trying to open your door because you were hurt. I wanted to open it because my mom taught me that's what you do for women especially ones you like."

"You like me?" she asked breathily with her other hand resting on my chest.

"Of course, I like you," I laughed unable to help

myself. "Why else would I have brought you back to my house to stay for a week or took you out tonight?"

Claire blushed and bit her bottom lip. I couldn't believe something so simple turned me on, but it did. A growl reverberated in my chest as my thumb slipped her lip out from between her teeth. Leaning down, I spoke quietly only enough for her ears. "You shouldn't do that."

She blinked up at me so innocently. She was so pure, and I knew I was going to tarnish her by being in her life, yet I couldn't help myself. Every moment of every day she was on my mind driving me to the point of madness if I didn't talk to her in some way. It was as if she'd put a spell on me and if that was the case, I didn't want the spell to ever break.

"Why?"

"Because it makes me want to do bad things to you. Very bad things and as much as I want to do those things to you, they'll have to wait until after dinner. I promised you I'd take you out and I intend to do so."

With her lips only a hairs breath away from my own, her words were a caress to the torment she inflicted upon me. "I like the sound of you doing bad things to me. Do you have to work tomorrow?" The last came out as a purr.

I was aware there were others around us, but I

didn't care. The only person in my world was Claire with her soft yet toned body pressed against mine.

"I do, but not until tomorrow night. We have plenty of time for me to have my wicked way with you." I nipped her bottom lip with each word making her breath speed up until she was all but panting. When she closed her eyes, I took her lips with mine. I hadn't planned on kissing her until we were both breathless, but when her arms wrapped around my neck and her tongue brushed against mine, all thought left me. I was back under her spell pressing my growing erection into her stomach as I devoured her mouth.

"Come on," a man behind us groaned loudly. We broke apart, panting. "Get a room or move with the line. Some of us want to eat tonight."

Claire's faced turned a gorgeous shade of pink that did nothing to help the situation in my pants, but I wasn't going to let my dick rule me. At least not until later when I had her in my bed and underneath me.

I stepped back but kept my arm around her waist as I moved us up in the line. You'd think we were next up with the way he interrupted us, but we still had a good ten people ahead of us. I decided now was a good time to tell Claire about the women who were getting beat up. Tell her would definitely keep my dick in line. She was quiet as I told her the news.

"Promise me you'll keep mace on you at all times

and your eyes peeled for any trouble. If you think you're in trouble call me."

Her eyes widened. "Okay, I promise. Do you really think someone might attack me?"

"Anything is possible," I answered her. Wanting to change the subject I decided to ask her about work. "Have you talked to your work yet about when you'll go back?"

Claire's shoulders slumped. "They think it's best if I wait until my cast is off so that means at least another four weeks." She looked down at her pink painted toenails. "I think I'm moving. It was either find a roommate or find a place I can afford. I talked to my friend, Aja and she said I could move in with her. Before you say anything, she lives in a better part of town. The apartment is nicer and it will be cheaper than what I'm now paying. We get along great so it should be an easy transition."

I wouldn't object to her moving to a nicer place, but still I had to ask. "Are you sure you want to move?"

"I don't really have much choice being without work for six weeks. It could be longer. Right now, they don't have me lined up until some comedy show at one of the casinos. There are always concerts in LA so I'm going to see if I can get a few of them to help out even if I have to deal with the commute."

"I never thought about it before but signing at a

concert is so awesome. Do you pick ones you know and like the music?" I wanted to go to one and see Claire do her thing.

"Normally, but if there are some requesting someone to do ASL and pay enough, I'll do them." She said quieter than normal. Was she ashamed she needed money? " It's not as easy, but sometimes I find a new band I didn't know of and like them."

Hugging her to my side, I rested my head on top of hers. "Hey, be proud of what you do. I am. I think it's awesome. You do what you have to do and if you need a police escort to any or all events, I'd be happy to take you."

"Thank you, Gage. I might take you up on your offer." She hugged my side a little tighter and stayed there until we were next in line. She bounced on her toes as she looked at the menu. "It smells so good," she moaned, making my dick twitch. "How have I never heard of this place before?"

"Because those that know of it like to keep it a secret. There's always a line and if everyone knew about it, we'd be here all-night waiting for tacos."

"Good point. I won't tell anyone. I can't decide what I want." She looked around at everyone who was sitting around the old plastic tables eating. "I think I'm going to try two different tacos."

"That's a good move. Maybe I'll get a few different

ones. It's been awhile since I didn't get my norm, but I can promise you even though each one is amazing you'll find a favorite or three."

"You really love this place, huh?"

"I really do. This was the first place Tate and I ate at when we moved here, and we knew we'd made the right decision after taking our first bite. Since then we come at least once a week. I'd choose Manny's over any other place for breakfast, lunch, or dinner."

"Gage, my man. How are you?" Manny shouted from behind the window. He wasn't who you'd expect to be working in a taco truck. If anything, you'd expect to see Manny out hitting the waves in Hawaii if he lost a hundred pounds or so.

"I'm good and you?"

"Great. Your brother was here last night and now you. Couldn't get any better than that. Are you going to have your usual?" His eyes rounded as I pulled Claire to my side. "You brought a date! She must be a very special lady."

"Very special," I agreed. "Manny this is Claire. Claire this is Manny, the owner and cook at this fine establishment."

Claire's mouth formed into an 'O'. "It's so nice to meet you. Gage can't stop talking about how amazing your tacos are and if they taste half as good as they smell they'll be amazing."

"A girl after my own heart," he clutched said heart dramatically making Claire giggle. "Gage, my man you better watch out or I might steal her away after she tries my tacos." I growled at him, but we both knew I didn't mean it.

"How do you know I haven't tried your tacos?" Claire asked from my side.

"Because I'd remember a pretty face like yours just like I remember his ugly mug," Manny grinned wide. Giving Claire his best smile. He was delusional if he thought he was going to steal her away from me.

Claire sputtered next to me "Ugly? I don't know who's buying your tacos if you think Gage is ugly."

"All the pretty boys eat here. Didn't you know?" Rapid firing his fingers at me, Manny winked. "Including the dynamic twin duo. Have you met Tate?" He leaned out the window and whispered loud enough for the next five people in line to hear him. "He's the better looking one if you ask me."

Claire only shrugged before linking her arm with mine. "To each their own. I happen to think Gage is the better looking one."

Manny scoffed and took out his order pad from the front pocket of his shirt. He was all business now. "What will you two have tonight?"

"It's been awhile since I've had anything but the

Spicy Matador so I'm going to have one of each and a beer."

"One of each?" They both asked at the same time with shock on their faces.

Claire turned to Manny as his pen hovered over the order slip. "Four's a lot. What's he thinking?"

I shook my head. Four was nothing. It was me on a light day.

"Are you watching your weight now that you've got a girlfriend?" He patted his overly round belly.

"Funny, but no. I had a late lunch and I'm not that hungry."

Claire stood with her mouth agape until Manny patted the hand she'd placed on the side of his truck. "How about you sweet thing?" He really needed to lay off before I lost it with all his flirting and every little jab. I'd never reacted this way for a woman before and I wasn't sure I liked it. I knew Manny didn't mean anything, but I couldn't help the rage building up inside of me.

"I'll have the...Zesty BBQ Pig," she grinned as if she'd made the right choice. There was no wrong choice at Manny's. That dude knew how to make killer tacos.

"Just one?" He asked with a frown.

"Um... I guess I'll have two. Make it two, Zesty BBQ Pigs and a water."

Manny's lips turned from a frown to a big smile. "Coming right up. Go find yourself a table and I'll personally bring them out to you."

Wrapping my arm around Claire's shoulders, we walked to the other side of the lot where a lone table sat with no one around. Sitting across the rickety picnic table from Claire, I watched as she took in the scene around us. More people were pulling into the parking lot, and there was a low hum from everyone's conversations. The best part was it sat a little higher than most of the city, so you got a great view with the mountains as a back drop.

Turning back to me she blushed when she found me staring at her. "Did you have any interesting calls… is that what you call them?"

"I know what you mean. I guess I had an interesting one. It was different for sure and I doubt it will be the last time we're out there." I only hoped the next time we were called out it wasn't too late.

Claire placed her elbows on the table and rested her chin on her hands giving me her undivided attention. "What happened?"

"She thought she saw someone outside and then someone left a dead cat on this women's doorstep. Her security lights have been going off every night." I took a deep breath knowing it in my gut that wasn't going to be the end for her.

"A dead cat," she gasped. "Who would do something like that?"

"A sicko and there's a lot of them out there. Earlier that night she'd been attacked outside of her place of work. She was lucky someone came upon them and saved her. He was injured and stupidly she brought him home when he refused to go to the hospital."

"Why is that stupid? She probably felt responsible for him getting injured."

"That's exactly why she did it, but he could be dangerous."

She leaned closer and whispered. "You don't think it was him who left the dead cat do you?"

"No," I shook my head. "It wasn't him."

"Did you get a bad vibe from him or something?" Her eyes got bigger at the thought.

I laughed at how eager she was. "This woman has a lot of money going by her house. It sits outside of town on the mountain and it's really fucking nice. I know there are a lot around here, but she's young and living the high life."

"So?" She shook her head. I was sure she thought I was overreacting and maybe I was.

"The guy she had staying at her house is homeless. He appeared to be harmless, but it still wasn't smart letting him stay at her house."

"He probably made her feel safe. He already saved

her once after all." One shoulder went up in a half shrug.

"That's easy for you to say when you haven't seen all the bad shit I have." I growled thinking of Claire doing the same thing and getting hurt in the process.

"Maybe you've grown too cynical by all the bad things you've seen. What if he's a perfectly nice guy? Won't you feel bad?"

"I can't feel bad because I want to protect the welfare of someone. And what if he's not this sweet guy and ends up killing her?" Maybe Tate was right about sharing our work with a girlfriend or wife. I was starting to think it was a bad idea.

"I don't know, Gage, but I hate it that you always think the worst about everyone and every situation."

"Not everyone or everything," I huffed.

My phone vibrated in my pants as Manny dropped our food off. I paid no attention to what he said as I read the text message from my brother.

Tate: **Another cops girlfriend was attacked tonight. It happened after she left from getting her hair done. Did you warn Claire?**

I felt dizzy knowing another woman had been attacked. Why was someone targeting the girlfriends and wives of police officers?

"Gage," Claire placed her hand over mine. "What's wrong? All the color drained from your face."

"Another woman was attacked. This time outside from where she gets her hair done. You're going to be careful right? Watching where you're going and keeping appraised of your surroundings."

"Of course, you tell me random women are being attacked all over the city; I'm going to keep an eye out. I don't want to get hurt again."

Maybe I should have told her the women were the wives and girlfriends of cops and not at all completely random, but I didn't want her to call whatever this was off before we ever got a chance. Only now it was me who was thinking she'd be better off in life without dating me.

10

GAGE

We'd been driving in silence for the last ten minutes. Silence surrounded us now and had since I received that text from my brother informing me another woman had been attacked all because she was dating a cop. She'd only been seeing him for a little over a week, so it made no sense how anyone knew about her. Worry gnawed at my gut at the possibility Claire might be attacked because of me.

To break the tension, I asked. "Did you have a good week?"

Claire shrugged and continued to look straight ahead. "It was nice getting back to work and I'm excited about the concert on Friday and Saturday, but I'm not looking forward to is going to LA for the weekend."

My entire body tensed knowing what she'd say

next. I wasn't prepared to disappoint her or hear the sadness in her voice. I was definitely not prepared for a black Camaro to pull out of the parking lot we were passing with its tires screeching as it fishtailed into traffic. It almost recovered until it clipped the back bumper of a city bus.

"What the hell Tate? Did you see that? He didn't stop or anything." Claire shrieked loud enough my ears rang.

"Siri, call 9-1-1," I barked out.

The phone call rang out through the speakers of my car. "9-1-1, what's your emergency?"

"This is officer Walker. Badge number nine, five, zero, three, seven. A black new model Camaro license plate six, tango, Romeo, lima, two, four, four hit city bus number eighteen traveling north on Cahulla a tenth of a mile passed Oceanside. Send out an ambulance and police. I'm in pursuit on the vehicle but send backup, I have a civilian in the car. Did you get all that?"

"Yes, sir. An ambulance and police are on their way."

My thumb hit the end button and then gripped the steering wheel so tight my knuckles turned white. I'd been trained to drive in this kind of circumstance, but with Claire in the car and her safety in my hands, I needed to be more diligent.

"We can't follow, Gage." My name came out as a high-pitched squeak.

"We have to otherwise he'll get away. Once backup catches up, we'll back off, but until then I'm sticking with this asshole."

"Fine," she huffed, throwing herself against her seat. "If you're going to make me be a part of this pursuit then you have to talk to me." I looked at her from the corner of my eye. Not daring to take my eyes off the road. "Why have you been acting so strange for the last… I want to say week since you've been slowly pulling away, but the truth is it's been almost a month." She chuckled darkly now looking out the passenger side window. "I don't understand. If you don't want to be with me…" her breath hitched. I looked over to see a lone tear stream down her cheek. I desperately wanted to wipe away her tear, but knew I couldn't. I had to keep my hands where they were. The knot that started to form in the last month grew. "If you don't want to be with me then just break up with me. It's the least you can do."

"Really, now?" I growled. I couldn't focus on a car chase and Claire asking me about why I'd been acting the way I had. Maybe if I'd been honest about the connection the women had to why they were being attacked, she'd understand. Instead I fought with myself every day with giving up Claire, to keeping her, and the danger I was putting her in if we were seen together. I'd been a dick this last month and I wasn't sure why she'd stayed with me, but damn was I happy she hadn't given up on me. I couldn't get enough of her.

"Yes, *now*. I know it's a bad time to say anything, but at least you can't run away," Claire gripped her seat until her knuckles turned white.

I gritted my teeth and hooked the car into the very left lane of traffic to avoid hitting a car who decided to pull out in front of us.

"I want you more than anything, Claire, but unfortunately there's nothing I can do right now to prove it to you."

She placed her hand on my knee and squeezed as she spoke barely above a whisper. "Actually, you can."

"Please enlighten me." I gritted out.

The Camaro decided to take that moment to drive on the left side of the road and into oncoming traffic. He was going to get himself killed and others if another officer didn't get on scene. If I had been alone, I *might* have followed in my own car, but no way in hell was I doing that with Claire with me.

"Come with me to LA, we'll have a nice weekend together—"

I couldn't listen to her talk about the amazing time

we'd have when it was never going to happen. "I can't get any time off this weekend. I'm sorry."

"Can't or won't?" She huffed and tightened her fingers around my leg.

"Claire, I can't, but maybe next time if you give me enough notice." Placing my hand over hers, I wove our fingers together. "I'm sorry, I can't go with you. There are others who have already asked for the weekend off and I'm not exactly the high man on the totem pole."

"I just don't understand why you've been acting so strange," she murmured dejectedly.

"I know you don't." And I should tell you.

Slipping my hand from hers, I put it back on my steering wheel in time to swerve around a slow-moving car. The Camaro jumped the median and slammed into a white SUV two cars in front of us. In turn, I had to move into the right lane to miss hitting the car in front of me and continue following.

"When are the police going to catch up? This guy…" Claire gasped as we watched the Camaro clip the back of a tow truck and then slam into an electrical pole.

Pulling up behind the Camaro, I parked and turned toward Claire. "Stay in the car and don't get out unless it's an emergency." Our eyes stayed locked as I took off my seatbelt and unlocked the glove compartment to slip out my gun and badge. Her eyes widened at the sight of my gun as she sucked her lips between her teeth. Stepping out of the car, I leaned down. "No getting out, okay?"

"Yes, Gage. I promise I won't get out of the car." She rolled her eyes but smiled at me.

Keeping my gun to my side, I made my way over to the driver's side of the now smoking Camaro. The windows were too tinted for me to see inside so I walked slowly up to the car. I didn't know if the driver had a gun or why he had kept going after hitting the bus, either way I was going to be cautious as I approached.

"Step out of the vehicle with your hands up," I ordered with my gun pointed at the driver's side window. I spotted no movement inside the car. It was possible the driver was unconscious after hitting the pole, still I kept my eyes and ears open. I called out my command again giving the driver another chance to step out and respond. Tapping my gun on the window, I still received no response and tried the door handle, but it was locked. I wasn't going to break out the window. I'd leave that for whoever showed up and responded.

Pulling my phone out of my pocket, I dialed 9-1-1 as I circled the car to see if any of the passenger side door were unlocked. "9-1-1, what's your emergency?" A female answered.

"This is officer Walker. Badge number nine, five, zero, three, seven. I called a little earlier about a car hitting a city bus."

"Yes, sir."

"I followed the perpetrator north on Cahulla and he has now stopped after hitting an electrical pole. I've approached the car with no response. I need you to send out an ambulance. We last passed Pasadena Drive about two tenths of a mile back. He's hit multiple cars along the way."

"Yes, sir we've had people calling after the car has hit them or witnessed it. Multiple cars should arrive in under two minutes to takeover."

<hr>

"I NEVER KNEW A CAR CHASE WAS SUCH AN aphrodisiac." Claire's hand slipped into the waistband of my pants and gripped my cock the moment we stepped inside my apartment.

I moaned at her touch and the way her hooded eyes looked up at me with a hunger I'd never seen before her. Her hunger ignited something deep inside of me on a primal level and I let it take over. In one movement, I pulled her little dress over her head and flung it to the ground before I carried her to my bedroom. We fell onto the bed with me braced on top of her. I slipped her panties and bra off in the next second before I crushed our mouths together in a lust filled kiss. My hand roamed up the side of her body and kneaded her full breast and tweaked her nipple with my fingers.

We came up for air both panting and smiling. Claire's hands ran up my back, her nails scraping my skin. "You need to take this off," she murmured in my ear before taking the lobe between her teeth and biting down.

Pulling away, I stood at the end of my bed, first taking off my shirt and then my jeans while never taking my eyes off Claire. "God, you're gorgeous. What are you doing with me?" I took my cock in my hand and stroked as I moved up the bed.

She blushed but kept her eyes on my moving hand. "You're the one that's gorgeous. Everywhere." She licked her lips.

"Do you want my cock in your pretty hot mouth?" I kneeled in front of her and continued to stroke my length.

"Yes, I want to taste you," she moaned.

Moving up the bed, I leaned back on my headboard and spread my legs wide. "Come here, baby. I want to see your pink lips wrap around my cock and suck me hard."

Claire crawled between my legs with hooded eyes,

her hands skimmed up my legs before she dipped down and swept her tongue around the head of my cock. Her hair fell around her face and I couldn't have that. I wanted to watch every single moment. Fisting her hair in my hand, I pulled it to the side and watched as she started to bob up and down. With each stroke she took more of me until I hit the back of her throat and swallowed.

"Fuck, you're driving me crazy. Your mouth feels so good," I moaned, fisting her hair harder. She looked up at me with her big gray eyes and smiled around my dick. It was what dreams were made of.

With each suck, lick and bob, Claire drove me wild. I felt like a teenage boy getting his cock sucked for the first time. I was ready to blow, and she'd only just started. She was good, too good, but nothing beat being deep inside of her. Thrusting my hips once more, I hit the back of her throat before I pulled her off and flipped her on her back. Lifting one leg, I placed it on my shoulder and plunge deep inside her hot, wet pussy.

Her eyes closed in ecstasy, back arching off the bed. "Gage," she called out, scraping her nails down my arm.

Leaning forward, I surged deeper and squeezed her tit. Loving the way her walls squeezed my cock when I hit deep inside of her. I kissed the arch of her foot and licked up her calf. She drove me wild. With each pump,

I had to thrust faster, harder. My skin slapped against her ass, my balls tightening.

"I want you to come with me," I grunted out as I held back my impending orgasm. My thumb found her clit and rubbed fast circles. Her pussy clamped down on my dick hard. I couldn't hold back any longer. Lifting her leg, I set it down to the bed. Leaning forward, I nuzzled and kissed her neck as she milked me of every last bit of cum inside my body.

Wrapping my arms around her, I moved to the side taking Claire with me. I breathed in her vanilla scent. My whole house smelled of her and I never wanted it to stop.

Lifting up to rest her chin on my chest, Claire smiled up at me. She looked drunk off sex and maybe she was. "We're awesome together," she laughed.

"We are. Are you ready to go again?" I felt my dick harden against my leg.

"Give a girl a few minutes," she giggled, but writhed against me.

A few hours later, I woke to my phone going off with Tate's tone and I rolled over to my side to check his message. When I read his words all the tension from the last month doubled, tightening in my chest. It was crippling. How was I possibly going to protect Claire?

***Tate:* Come over as soon as you can. There's been another one.**

Claire yawned. "Is everything okay?"

I shook my head as I typed out a message.

"Do you want to talk about it?" She asked on another yawn, her voice concerned.

I looked at my phone and read the message again. I couldn't let anything happen to Claire and the only way I saw a way to do that was to no longer see her.

She must have felt the shift in the air. Maybe my body tensed up. I'm not sure what happened, but I was already hating myself. I watched as Claire pulled away from my side and sat on the other side of the bed. She hugged her knees to her chest while tears streamed down her flushed cheeks. "You can't keep pulling away from me, Gage. I won't let you use me like that. Until you figure out whatever's going on in that head of yours, I think it's best if we don't see each other again."

I was thinking she was right.

I watched with a dead heart as she grabbed her bra and panties and left the room. I didn't try to stop her even when I heard the front door slam.

11

———

GAGE

One Month Later

MY LEFT KNEE BOUNCED THE ENTIRE DRIVE UP TO LA. Of course, I started out a little too late and hit traffic. I didn't want to be late to the concert, but it was inevitable. I'd be lucky to arrive before it was over with the rate traffic was moving. It had been a month since Claire walked out my door and I did nothing to stop her. I'd barely slept or ate in that time. In such a short amount of time, she worked her way under my skin, and I didn't think I'd ever get over her. I was desperate to feast my eyes on her even if she didn't want to ever see me again. I needed to see her one last time.

When I called Claire's work, I was surprised that most of her jobs were in LA. Luckily, I had a couple of days off that coincided with one of her jobs. Tate had surprisingly been nudging me to talk to Claire. He saw how miserable I was for letting her walk away and even though I was depressed, I knew Claire was safe because we'd broken up.

After almost five hours, I finally made it to my hotel that was a short walk to the Staples Center and found a parking place. After a quick check-in, I was anxious after all this time to see Claire. I half walked; half jogged down the sidewalk until I got inside. Trying to hurry, I pulled up my ticket on my phone and tried to flash it as I went by one of the workers.

"Excuse me, sir." A big burly guy who looked like he would eat me for dinner if I didn't stop threw his arm out in front of me. I did what any sane man would do. I stopped. "I need to scan your ticket before you can go through."

Tapping my phone to bring my ticket up again, I held it out with a fake smile on my face. I didn't need to be an asshole and get kicked out before I even saw her. I swore he took his time as he repeatedly tried to scan my phone. Of course, I was stopped when I was in a hurry. Didn't they know I was in a hurry and needed to see my woman? Or who used be my woman.

"Can you adjust your brightness, sir? My scanner isn't picking up your ticket." His lips twitched. I knew it! He was delaying me on purpose. There was no one else around because the concert had started over two hours ago.

Turning the brightness to my phone all the way up, I held it out one last time. When it finally scanned, the guy put his sweaty hand on my shoulder and gave it a pat. "Go get her," he yelled after I took off.

I swear I heard them laughing at me as I sprinted toward my seat. I wasn't sure where Claire would be, but I'd gotten a seat as close to the floor as possible to some dude I'd never heard of. Rap music wasn't my thing, but I'd do anything to see Claire again and win her back.

Loud music blasted me the closer I got. How had I forgot my earplugs? Instead of letting the music get to me, I concentrated on finding my seat and Claire. After finding my seat, I stood with the rest of the crowd and scanned the area for a red headed beauty. God must have been looking down on me or karma was starting to work in my favor because after only thirty-seconds I found Claire on the floor thirty feet away from me.

I wanted the concert to be over so that I could get her attention. I wouldn't interrupt her work and possibly get her fired. Instead I stood, tuned out the music, and stared at her like a psycho. Even though her hands and body were moving to the beat there was a cloud of melancholy that surrounded her. The pit in my stomach grew knowing that I could very well be the reason she looked so down. Had Claire been a mess like me for the last month? She must have felt someone staring at her because she looked in my direction and faltered. Her eyes widened and her mouth gaped open, but she quickly recovered and started signing again.

Standing in awe, I watched her hands and the group of people in front of her. Never before meeting Claire did, I think someone who was deaf would go to a concert. I didn't even know there were ASL interpreters for music events until I met Claire.

Before Claire I thought I was happy. I thought my life was fulfilled with my job, my brother, and being a bachelor, but one smile from her, and I was ready to change everything for her to be in my life and in my bed. I didn't care that she was younger or what people would say. Since we'd been apart whoever was attacking and beating up the girlfriend's and wives of cops had stopped. Now I could be with Claire and she'd be safe. I only hoped she accepted my apology once I explained to her why I'd acted the way I had.

The rest of the concert was spent with my eyes glued to Claire. I looked her up and down to see if anything else had changed besides her cast being off. She looked a little thinner than she had a month ago.

She was dressed in dark jeans that hugged her ass in the most delicious way and a black tank top with Chucks on her feet.

Perfection.

As the concert started to end with its second encore, I wasn't sure what my next move would be. There were thousands of people at the venue and as soon as everyone started to move, I'd lose Claire. As if she knew what I was thinking, Claire held up her phone waving it in the air right before a swarm of people engulfed her. Pulling my phone out, I was glad I had the forethought to charge it on my way to the concert otherwise it would probably be dead. Looking down my battery life was only at fifteen percent. For some reason in the last few months, my phone had started to lose battery life at an insane pace. I left it on the charger most of the time not caring. I needed a new one, but with the funk I'd been in since letting Claire leave, I'd done nothing, but work and drink.

Pulling up my messages, I knew I needed to quickly send her a location to meet before my phone died and we never found each other. If I had to, I'd look for her all night long.

Tate: *Can you meet me outside the front doors on the west side?*

Making my way outside, I kept my phone in my

hand hoping to feel it vibrate with a message from Claire. Once out in the open, I started to get worried when I hadn't heard from her. Maybe her phone was dead and that's why she was waving it at me. A million scenarios went through my head at why I hadn't gotten a text yet. Never in my life had I been more nervous than I was waiting to see if I'd hear from her. My plan was to go where I'd messaged her to meet and then work from there. If she didn't meet with me, I knew I'd be devastated.

Cool air hit my face the moment I stepped outside. I felt like I could finally breathe after being in the hot, humid building for the last hour. Moving to the west side of the building, I leaned up against the wall while I waited to see which direction my life would turn. I had to tamp down the urge to pace or tap my foot. It was good I was tall and had been trained to observe and catch stuff the untrained eye wouldn't see. I wasn't as good as Tate, but I wasn't bad, and I think it gave me an advantage while looking for Claire.

After about twenty minutes, Claire came rushing around a corner bumping into a group of guys. I saw red as one of the guys grabbed her by the arms. At first it seemed he was trying to be helpful so she didn't fall down, but I saw Claire try to step away, but couldn't. He was tall and built but he had nothing on me, but it was enough to intimidate her. Their glassy eyes indicated they were drunk and most likely ready to start trouble. All the guys were laughing as her faced turned redder by the second.

Pushing my way through the crowd on the sidewalk in three easy strides, I stepped up behind Claire and grasped her waist. Her body stiffened against my touch as she tried to pull away from the man holding her arms. "Let go of the woman," I warned. Hearing my voice, Claire's body melted against mine and a small knot of tension released inside of me.

Looking me up and down their eyes widened. Instantly the douchebags hands dropped, and I wrapped an arm around Claire, pulling her tight to my body. I wanted to pump my chest and tell them all to step back from my woman but refrained myself. I was sure Claire wouldn't appreciate it and I didn't need anything more that would sore her from me.

"You ready to get out of here?" I asked her while keeping my eye on the group of guys. They took a step back, but not enough for my liking. Taking her hand in mine, I directed us around a large group of teenage girls squealing and headed down the sidewalk. Another knot loosened as we walked.

Claire pulled her hand from mine, stopping us on the busy sidewalk. When I looked back, she was standing with her hands on her hips and glaring up at me. "What do you think you're doing?"

"What are you doing?" I barked back a little too harshly by her wide eyes. Taking a deep breath, I closed my eyes and tried to relax. *Just talk to her.* "I'm sorry," I softened my tone. "I only wanted to get away from all this." I indicated all the people who had stopped to stare at us.

"Why?" She gritted out, her hand back on her hips.

"To talk and explain about why I acted the way I did. Please, Claire come with me. I'll take you anywhere you want to go."

She looked around at the crowd we'd drawn and wrapped her arms around herself. Claire might be young, but she'd never been self-conscience. Had I done this to her?

"Fine, but don't hold my hand." She jutted her chin up, eyes blazing, showing the strong girl she was.

"I won't hold your hand unless you ask," I promised. "Where's your car?"

"At my hotel. I took an Uber so I wouldn't have to deal with traffic. Where's your car?" She asked looking around. It seemed she didn't realize I was extremely late for the concert otherwise I never would have gotten a parking place anywhere near here unless I used the valet. There was no way I was letting those punks drive my car.

"I parked it at my hotel. I'm staying at the Luxe," I pointed in the direction I was staying. "We can go there."

Her upper body tensed as she kept pace with me. "Um… I don't know if that's such a good idea."

Looking down at her as we walked in the direction of my hotel, I smirked at her. "Are you afraid to be alone with me?"

"Yeah, I am. I can't let my attraction to you deter my better judgement. You hurt me once, I won't let you do it again."

My smirk vanished and it took everything in me to stop myself from touching her. I wanted to hold her hand or wrap my arms around her. "Fair enough. My room is a suite with a sitting room, I promise not to try anything untoward if you agree to come up and let me talk."

"Do I get to do any of the talking?" She sassed back making my dick twitch.

"After I explain what happened."

"Then my all means please lead the way. I can't wait to hear what you have to say but then you're going to listen to me." Her voice shook and I wasn't sure if it was from anger, sadness, or a little bit of both. If I had to guess, it was a combination of the two.

I'd listen to whatever she had to say. I was thankful she'd agreed to talk to me after I showed up unannounced where she was working for the night. It could have been a lot worse.

We were quiet for the short walk to the hotel. It only took a couple of minutes, but the entire time I could feel the tension radiating from her only a foot away. I tried to give Claire her space in the elevator by standing on the other side until three couples stumbled in laughing and hanging all over each other. Immediately I moved to her side but kept my promise to keep my hands to myself. She never said I couldn't look at her, so I stared down at her as we waited for my floor.

Once in my room, I wanted to pounce. Instead I watched as she took in the room. It was nice and where I hoped we'd both be staying for the weekend otherwise I wouldn't have splurged.

"This is… nice. Much better than the room I was put up in." She shivered as if the thought of her room gave her the heebie-jeebies. I would hate for her to spend her own money, but if someone else was paying and it wasn't nice maybe Claire staying with me was more in the cards than I thought. The room was nice and modern with a big king size bed and a TV hanging on the wall in the other room. A frosted door closed the small living area they called a parlor, off from the bedroom and bathroom.

"You can stay here if you want," I blurted out. I'd

meant to ask her once I'd explained everything not before.

She'd been about to sit down on the couch but shot up and started heading for the door. "I knew I shouldn't have come. You only want one thing and I'm not going to go there with you. If you want someone to screw all you need to do is step out onto the street, and you'll have girls flocking toward you. You don't need me." Claire was at the door with her hand on the door knob when I stopped her by blocking her way. There was no way she was getting around me.

"That's not what I want. I mean yeah of course; I want to have sex with you…" I stopped at the dark look that came across her face. If looks could kill, I'd be dead with a hundred daggers sticking out of me. "But most importantly I want to explain myself. I need to tell you why I started to pull away."

"Fine," she huffed and stomped over to the couch. Sitting down Claire pointedly looked over at the chair across from her. I guess I wouldn't be sitting by her on the couch. Taking my place on the chair, I stretched my legs out in front of me, but then sat up with my elbows on my knees.

"Now that I've got you here, I'm… nervous." All of a sudden, I had a feeling this very well might not go the way I'd hoped. "I know what I did was wrong, and I should have talked to you," I chuckled darkly. "I was stupid—"

"Oh, you think?" She laughed without humor.

I gave her a pointed look. She'd promised to hear me out. Claire made the motion of zipping her lips closed and throwing away the key.

"As I was saying I was stupid. I was afraid if I told you why I was acting the way I was then you'd leave me and then… it happened anyway." I scrubbed my hands through my hair and down my face. This was harder than I thought it was going to be. I knew Claire would be mad, but I didn't expect to be able to feel her anger directed toward me.

"Just tell me why you'd be so warm and… loving and then a little later you'd shut down. You never wanted to go out on dates… were, no," she shook her head. "Are you ashamed of me? To be seen with me?" Her breath hitched on the last word.

"No," I shot up and moved to kneel on the floor beside her. There was a table in the way, so I had to push it to the side to get to her. My hands hovered over hers unable to touch her unless she gave me permission. I waited and waited, but she never gave me the permission I needed. Hanging my head, I closed my eyes and continued. "Do you remember when I told you there had been a string of women who'd been beaten and attacked around Oasis?"

"Yes, what does that have to do with anything? I was safe and careful everywhere I went. I still am. Nothing—"

Looking up at her, I let Claire see how sorry I was for lying to her. "I didn't tell you everything. I thought if I did, I'd never see you again."

"What didn't you tell me, Gage?" She asked softly. One hand lifted as if she was going to touch me but it fell back into her lap.

"It wasn't random women who were being assaulted. They were the girlfriend's and wives of cops," I swallowed roughly at finally getting the truth out. I felt better for telling her the truth, but I wasn't sure she'd forgive me or take me back. "I was scared to death that if we were seen together out in public you'd be targeted. I'm sorry I didn't tell you everything. I knew when you left that day it was for the best, but I've thought about you every single day since the moment you left. You're all I can think about day or night."

"I... I would have been safer if you'd told me and I'd like to think that I wouldn't have broken up with you, but I can't say since you never gave me the chance. What's changed now? Why are you here? Why did you track me down in LA? So, you could get this burden off your chest?"

"I wanted to see you work. When you asked me to come before I did want to, and I did *try* but couldn't get off. I wasn't making excuses. I loved watching you out there. You're absolutely amazing. You know there might be times the police station might need to hire you as an interpreter. Would you be open to doing that?"

"I can always use the money," She tilted her head to the side. "Is that all you wanted to say?"

"I have so much to say, but I don't know what I want to say at the same time. You scare me, Claire. I've never met a woman like you that I wanted to open up to. I've never told anyone how growing up with two different colored eyes made me feel like a freak. I mean Tate knew, but he doesn't count. I can't hide anything from him." I stood and started to pace in front of her. "I hated pushing you away and at first I didn't mean to. I'd find out about another woman being brutally beat up and I'd get so scared you'd be next. The day you left," she nodded her head and clenched her hands together remembering that day with me. "I got a message when we were in bed together and it was Tate. It was vague. All he said was there was another one and to come over as soon as I could." I stopped and looked down at her. Her eyes were filled with unshed tears. "I freaked out that you'd be next and then you left. I didn't want it, but I knew you'd be safe, so I let you go." Shaking my head, I slid down the wall and sat on the floor directing across from her. "When I got to Tate's house, I found out it wasn't a woman who'd been beaten up but killed. Tate has been working on what is now been dubbed the Scarlett Killer case and has asked me to help him go over evidence a couple of times to have new eyes on it. It had nothing to do with someone possibly hiring you."

Claire touched her red locks and chewed on the corner of her mouth. "Wow. I need a couple of minutes to think. That was a lot and while it does explain why you acted the way you did, I'm not—"

"I promise to always be honest with you from here on out if you take me back," I interrupted. "I've been a mess since I let you walk out of my life. I can't sleep or eat. I won't be whole again until I have you back in my life."

Claire got up and for a brief moment I thought she was coming to me, but instead she moved over to look out the window. I'd told her everything and now the ball was in her court. I could do nothing but watch her as Claire stared out the window. My life hung in the balance of her decision. I knew I'd never get over her if I had to let her go.

"Do you promise to talk to me if you think I'm in danger and we can talk about it?" She asked still looking out the window. Her shoulders were bunched up by her ears.

Shooting up to my feet, my heart raced. "I promise on everything that's holy. I promise on my mom and

Tate; I won't push you away and I'll tell you everything unless it's classified."

Claire turned around tears streaming down her face and I couldn't hold back any longer. I went to her and pulled her into my arms, and hugged her for long minutes breathing her in. I loved her vanilla scent and once it disappeared from my apartment, I'd nearly lost it. Now she was back in my life and I wasn't going to let her go. "Is this okay? I know I said I'd wait until you gave me permission, but I couldn't stand seeing you cry."

"Yes," she croaked out. Her head resting on my chest felt like the best gift in the world. "It's perfect. Being in your arms feels like home." Pulling back, Claire looked up at me and cupped my face in her tiny hands. "I've missed you and your beautiful eyes."

Claire was the only person to ever love my eyes besides my mother. It healed a part of me that had been broken since I was a child.

Dipping down I took her mouth in a desperate kiss and pulled her body flush against mine. It had been too long since I'd felt her touch. Our kiss was one of long-ing, apology, acceptance, and passion. Her hands went under my shirt, skating over my abs; her nails scraped against my skin. With each touch, I growled and kissed her deeper. I wanted to devour her.

Picking her up, I kissed and nibbled down her neck

as I walked us to the bedroom. She tasted better than ever before and I couldn't wait to feast on her body all night long. Pulling away from her delectable neck, I bit her earlobe and growled. "I need to be inside you now. I promise I'll worship your body for the rest of the night afterwards."

"Only if you let me worship you as well," she panted, grinding down on my denim covered erection.

Not wasting any time, I pushed her up against the wall and ripped her shirt over her head. Pulling her bra down, I took her breast into my mouth and laved at her rosy nipple until it was diamond hard while unbuttoning her jeans and shimmying them down her toned legs. It was a bit tricky, but I didn't care. I couldn't put her down with the insatiable need to feel her body against mine.

"What's taking you so long?" Claire giggled as I unzipped my pants and pulled my cock out.

"I'll give you something to laugh about." I lined up my dick with her entrance and slammed inside. Being deep inside of her felt like home. I was where I belonged.

Claire gasped, throwing her head back and started to move up and down my shaft. She was just as hungry for me as I was for her. Cupping the back of her head, I anchored her in place. With my hands on her hips, I set a blurring pace. I'd never been so lost in a woman in my life. My mouth slanted over hers as our tongues entwined and pleasure coursed through my body. My balls tightened with each moan from Claire.

With one final thrust, I stilled deep inside. Moaning into the side of Claire's neck, I wrapped my arms around her and held her close as tremors wracked her body and her sweet pussy continued to milk my cock.

Tightening my arms around her, I stepped away from the wall and carried Claire to the bed. Laying her down, I crawled in beside her and pulled her on top of me. She kissed my chest and laid her head in the crook of my neck and shoulder and nuzzled in. The moment was perfect, and I never wanted the night to end.

"I know this is probably the worst possible time to tell you this." I ran my hand from her hair down her back and then up again. "But I can't wait any longer. This month without you has been torture and I don't want to hold back with you any longer."

Lifting her head up to rest her chin on my chest, she softly asked. "What is it?"

"I never told anyone this but family that's probably why I'm shit at telling you." Cupping her cheek, I trailed my thumb over her smooth skin. "I love you, Claire."

Claire blinked at me in disbelief before a smile bloomed across her gorgeous and flushed face. "I love you too, Gage."

No better words had been spoken. Gripping her hips, I pulled her up and kissed her until the world fell away.

If you loved Gage and Claire, I think you'll love Bodhi and Coco in Secret Admirer.

Want to stay in the know? Sign up for my newsletter for all my releases, sales, and exclusive giveaways.

Did you enjoy The Model? If so, please consider leaving a review on Goodreads, Amazon, or BookBub. Reviews mean the world to authors especially to authors who are starting out. You can help get your favorite books into the hands of new readers.
I'd appreciate your help in spreading the word and it will only take a moment to leave a quick review. It can be as short or as long as you like. Your review could be the deciding factor or whether or not someone else buys my book.

To stay up to date on all my exclusive bonus scenes, releases, and sales, subscribe to my newsletter.
http://bit.ly/HarlowLayneNL

WANT MORE GAGE AND CLAIRE?

Want more Tate and Claire? You'll see much more of them in Tate's book. Find out who's the killer that's had Tate tirelessly working.

ABOUT HARLOW

Indie Author. Romance Writer. Reader. Mom. Wife. Dog Lover. Addicted to all things Happily Ever After and Amazon.

Harlow Layne is a hopeless romantic who writes sweet and sexy alpha males who will make you swoon.

Harlow wrote fanfiction for years before she decided to try her hand at a story that had been swimming in her head for years.

When Harlow's not writing you'll find her online shopping on Amazon, Facebook, or Instagram, reading, or hanging out with her family and two dogs.

ALSO BY HARLOW LAYNE

<u>Fairlane Series - Small Town Romance</u>

With Love, Alex

Hollywood Redemption - Single Parent

Hollywood Fairytale - Single Parent, Suspense

Unsteady in Love - Second Chance, Military

Kiss Me - Holiday, Insta-Love

Fearless to Love - Insta- Love

<u>Love is Blind Series- Reverse Age Gap Romance</u>

Intern - Office Romance

The Model - Workplace Romance

The Bosun - Coming Spring 2021

<u>Hidden Oasis Series</u>

Secret Admirer - Damsel in Distress, Opposites Attract, Suspense

<u>Worlds</u>

Cocky Suit - RomCom, Office, Interracial

Risk - Forbidden, Sports

Affinity - Part of the Fairlane Series - Accidental Marriage, Enemies-to-Lovers

Willow Bay Series - Forbidden

Away Game - MM, Bully - February 4, 2021

Anthologies

Heard It In a Love Song - An LGBT+ Anthology

All profits go to charity.